Sherlock Holmes – The Baker Street Legacy

Another collection of previously unknown cases from the extraordinary career of Mr. Sherlock Holmes

Mark Mower

Paperback ISBN 9781787054325
ePub ISBN 9781787054332
PDF ISBN 9781787054349

Published by MX Publishing
335 Princess Park Manor, Royal Drive,
London, N11 3GX
www.mxpublishing.co.uk
Cover design by Brian Belanger
www.belangerbooks.com and www.redbubble.com/people/zhahadun

Contents

The Great Detective (by Rosie Mower)

Sherlock Holmes travels by

Hansom cabs.

Evidence reveals the culprit,

Rooms are full of clues,

Lestrade is not impressed.

Only Watson knows his methods,

Carefully stalking the guilty -

Killers beware!

Home is 221b

On Baker Street,

London.

Moriarty is his arch-enemy –

Evil deeds he carries out.

Someday, Holmes will defeat him...

Preface

Dear readers - Following the successful publication of *The Baker Street Case-Files* some two years ago, you have once again challenged me to gather together another selection of previously unknown Holmes and Watson cases from the prized collection of stories I inherited from my uncle in 1939. This is my response to your polite requests – *The Baker Street Legacy*.

There appears to be a distinct mood of optimism in Britain as I write this, and some developments which I am sure Holmes and Watson would have approved of. In January, the railway industry – which provided a backdrop and the essentials means of travel in so many of the pair's cases – was nationalised, to become *British Railways*. Last month, our *National Health Service* began to function, providing universal medical treatment, free at the point of use, for every British citizen – something that both I and my uncle had long campaigned for. And in the last couple of weeks, we have seen the glorious spectacle of the London Summer Olympics and Stoke Mandeville Games at Wembley, the first such international events to be held since 1936. Holmes once said that amateur sport was "*...the best and soundest thing in England.*" How gratified he would have been to see our athletes competing against many from overseas in what the King has described as "*keen but friendly rivalry.*"

The stories I have chosen for this volume are more overlooked gems. The first in the collection, *A Day at the Races*, is set in 1880, before my uncle had become the chief chronicler of the Great Detective's work. *The French Affair* is a fascinating tale set in that period beyond 1891 when the world was led to believe that Holmes had died at the Reichenbach Falls grappling with the villainous Professor Moriarty. From the allure of *The Fashionably Dressed Girl* to the operation of *The Influence Machine*, there is, as always, much to entertain and enthral us.

I am pleased to say that with the release of this book I have already begun to contemplate a further, perhaps final, volume – such is the continued fascination with those two men who once occupied that setting we have come to know and love as 221B Baker Street.

As ever: *"The game is afoot!"*

Christopher Henry Watson, MD

Bexley Heath, Kent – 15th August 1948

1. A Day at the Races

It had long been a habit of mine to cast off the shackles of my professional life and to make the annual pilgrimage to Epsom Downs in order to meet up with a group of old student friends from Pembroke College, Oxford. Our get-together at the Derby Stakes was predicated on the enduring friendship that we still enjoyed and the chance to indulge in a day of mirth, gambling and drinking. And it was in this most unlikely of settings that I first encountered Mr. Sherlock Holmes.

It was on a Wednesday in the early part of June 1880 that my story began. That afternoon I had enjoyed some small success, having placed my usual stake of one guinea on the nose of the Duke of Westminster's thoroughbred *Bend Or,* ridden at that time by the immensely talented Fred Archer. Having collected my winnings, I readily agreed to buy our party of eight some champagne in a marquee near the Tattenham Corner end of Epsom Fair. While seating ourselves around a large trestle table just inside the canopy, my dear friend Cedric Stone began to gesticulate wildly in the direction of a tall, thin-looking fellow, who sat alone at one of the tables close to the main bar. With a wholehearted invitation to join us, the young man pulled up a chair and was soon introduced to our boisterous party. Stone explained that our guest was a private detective from London who had recently assisted his father in recovering a valuable diamond ring from the clutches of a well-known gentleman thief. To a further round of loud cheers and the evident embarrassment of the man, we welcomed Holmes to the group and insisted that he partake of some refreshment with us.

It was gloriously hot and sunny that afternoon and despite the hustle and bustle of the busy marquee, Holmes soon looked to be relaxed in our company. I guessed he was still in his twenties and some five or six years younger than most of us. Gaunt and eagle-eyed, in a smartly tailored Norfolk jacket, cap and breeches, I found him to be observant, direct and witty, and charming in his general manner. There was no doubting his keen intelligence and he seemed conversant on most subjects – including earlier Derby winners – explaining that he and his brother regularly attended the Classics. However, he was quick to point out that his visit to the Derby that year had nothing to do with his fondness for the turf. In fact, he had just completed a case linked to horseracing of which he could say no more.

Within an hour or so, our party began to disperse, some colleagues saying their goodbyes before returning to London or Oxford, and a couple arranging to travel further afield. That left just Cedric and I in the company of Holmes, who seemed keen to stick with us and head for a quieter part of the fair. A short time later, we were seated at a small wooden table in a more convivial setting, enjoying a pot of tea and a thick slice of Madeira cake with the gentle sound of accordion music being played close by.

"Tell me, Mr. Hughes, what made you become a school master, when your real passion in life appears to be the study of astronomy?"

Holmes's question caught me by surprise and my hand moved instinctively to the lapel badge of the Royal Astronomical Society that I always wore on any formal or social occasion. I returned a grin and answered: "I am indeed a fellow of the Royal Society – but more of an amateur star-gazer than a serious scientist. My father bought me my first telescope when I was eight years old and I have never lost the fascination for staring into the great unknown. Is it a field of study that interests you?"

Holmes snorted rather dismissively. "No, I can't say that it is. My focus has always been on more earthly matters."

"Now, that is a shame. The society thrives on the keen instincts and observational talents of its members. You don't seem to miss much at all and would be well equipped looking through the lens of a reflecting telescope. But tell me, how did you know that I was a school master? Has Cedric been briefing you?"

Cedric, who was sitting opposite me, laughed and held up his arms. "Not guilty, my Lord! You are now discovering why Mr. Holmes is such a well-regarded detective, Geraint."

"I see. Well I am a master – or *beak* as the boys like to refer to us – at Harrow. I teach mathematics and have been in the post since leaving university. I have no great ambitions, so an easy life teaching at my former school seemed preferable to the rigours, demands and uncertainties of a scientific career. In short, I suppose I am by nature somewhat slothful, Mr. Holmes. But I am still at a loss to know how you could have guessed my profession."

"I rarely, if ever, resort to guesswork, Mr. Hughes. I follow a rudimentary, yet generally effective, pattern of observational analysis – placing one or two discernible facts together – to form a working hypothesis. The more facts and data I gather, the stronger becomes my supposition. In your case, the clues were overwhelming."

I was at once both intrigued and vexed by his words. *Was the course of my life so obviously transparent?*

"I think you must carry on and put poor Geraint out of his misery, Mr. Holmes!" This time it was Cedric who spoke, looking every bit as keen as I was to hear more.

Holmes sat forward in his chair, his eyes fixed firmly on mine. "Your general demeanour speaks of someone used to the hubbub of a common room or school refectory. In the marquee you were completely unfazed by the noise and commotion around you. I watched you take the lead in shepherding your friends into the tent, pointing and issuing directions and ensuring that you were the last in, so as to leave no one behind. Ever the school master, your voice was clear and commanding, yet never close to a shout. Your attire attests to your chosen profession – a tweed frock coat, with leather padding on the elbows to minimise the wear as you work away at your desk and a pair of sleeve garters on that keenly starched white shirt. Other tell-tale signs merely add to the whole; the ink stains on your left thumb and forefinger, the wooden ruler tucked within an inside pocket and the eye glasses that you rely upon to read, yet hide within your top pocket for reasons of vanity. The profession suits your bachelor status, but I suspect that you have not given up all hope of marrying one day."

It was a singular performance which prompted both Cedric and me to applaud, neither of us knowing what to say as a direct response. I felt no slight at the remarks and at once realised that his extraordinary talents set him apart, though I had no notion then that he would become the world-renowned investigator we know today. His mention of my bachelor status triggered a fresh set of thoughts which I then felt I had to share with the detective.

"You will no doubt think me presumptuous, Mr. Holmes, but since I have now seen you at work, there is a conundrum I am currently faced with, on which I would value your professional opinion. Clearly, I would not expect you to labour without recompense, so I would be happy to pay you a reasonable fee for any help you can provide."

Holmes nodded, sat back in his chair and brought his right index finger up to his thin lips while contemplating the proposition. "Without any offence to you, sir, I would prefer to hear the nature of the conundrum first, before I commit to provide any assistance – particularly if the matter you refer to concerns a young woman."

For a second time, Holmes had succeeded in leaving me speechless. Once more, Cedric intervened on my behalf. "There is certainly no fooling you, Mr. Holmes. Geraint has already shared with me the facts of the matter I believe he is about to disclose – it is a pretty puzzle and does indeed concern an even prettier young lady."

Holmes remained impassive, glancing casually in the direction of the accordion players before focusing once more on my expectant face. "The involuntary dilation of your pupils when I mentioned your hopes of marrying one day, betrayed your emotional state. I will gladly listen to what you have to say, but must point out that I generally avoid cases of a matrimonial or romantic nature."

I was quick to respond. "That is understood. But I think you will find the facts of this case a little more engaging."

A quick nod from the detective suggested that he was in agreement, and with this as a sufficient inducement, I then began my narrative.

"A little over a year ago I was called into the study of the Headmaster, the Reverend Henry Butler, with an announcement that he had a mission for me. He is an affable fellow, but one who expects his staff to rise to any particular challenges they are set. And despite my initial reservations about any scheme or plan he had in mind, I was subsequently reassured to learn that the task itself appeared to be relatively straightforward.

"The school had received a letter from a Mr. Kenneth Buttenshaw, a northern industrialist who has established a successful cloth-making business in Darlington. The factory owner had desires for his only son, Simon Buttenshaw, to receive a gentleman's education, so was keen to pay for him to attend Harrow before taking on a substantive role within the family business. In support of his son's admission, Buttenshaw indicated that he was not only willing to pay the regular termly fees required for a pupil from outside the Harrow area, but would also be prepared to grant the school a bursary of some two thousand pounds a year for the time the boy remained in education.

"I should make it clear, Mr. Holmes, that the Reverend Butler is a reforming headmaster, who has been open with the school governing board in indicating that greater efforts should be made to attract more fee-paying pupils. He liked the tone of Buttenshaw's letter, felt that the opportunity should not be overlooked and instructed me to travel up to County Durham to meet the family and discuss the arrangements for admitting the new pupil after the Easter term. In short, I made the journey to the Buttenshaw's substantial home on the outskirts of Darlington in the early part of April last year and dealt with all of the paperwork necessary to receive the boy. Simon was enrolled within the school some weeks later and has, since that time, proved to be an exemplary pupil. He is thirteen years of age and has a keen grasp of science, a flair for mathematics and a clear passion for classical literature."

Holmes interjected. "And yet, I fear that your concern or conundrum has little to do with the boy or his admission to the school?"

"No, indeed – that much has been straightforward. But perhaps I should say more about my experience in meeting the Buttenshaw family. The father is a short greying man of some girth, with a direct and witty line of banter. I would say that he is around sixty-five years of age and is a widower – his much younger wife having died some years ago from English cholera. He appears to have no pretensions, is open and honest in admitting that he has come from humble stock, but is equally forthright in wanting to ensure that his two children benefit from all of the wealth and opportunities his business has created. Alongside Simon, he has a daughter, Sophia, who is now twenty-two. She dotes on her father and brother and, as well as appearing to run their house, takes a very active role in the administration of the business."

Holmes cut in again: "The young lady that you have become so attached to, I take it?"

I felt my face redden. "There is no denying it. I am completely smitten with Miss Buttenshaw. From the moment I met her that day, I have entertained only one notion, that we might at some point announce our engagement and marry. That hope may now have been extinguished."

The detective glanced at me quizzically. "Mr. Hughes, I have no wish to be dismissive, but as yet, have heard nothing to suggest that there is any mystery or intrigue within this affair. However, I would be grateful if you could outline the sequence of events that has led to Miss Buttenshaw announcing recently that she no longer wishes you to court her."

I was a little perturbed at his brusque manner but realised that I had, to that point, made my narration sound like a traditional and gushing tale of unrequited love. "I apologise, Mr. Holmes. You can be forgiven for believing that ours was a short-lived romance which Sophia has now brought to a point of some conclusion. But the matter is not as simple as that, and I believe strongly that there are other forces at work here, the nature of which I have not yet determined. I am not prepared to give up on Sophia and would willingly pay you a king's ransom to know why she has recently broken off all communications with me."

"If I am to be of any assistance in this matter, I must have further details," exclaimed Holmes, the veins on the side of his head seeming suddenly very pronounced. "Perhaps you could tell me more about that first encounter and the way that the courtship developed?"

"I am not sure what to tell you and what to leave out," I replied, eager to assist. "When I arrived at the house I was shown into the drawing room by one of the household staff and introduced to young Simon. He is a likeable lad, quiet and well-mannered, who told me that he relished the prospect of attending Harrow, but admitted that he would miss his family. As a former boarder myself, I told him that was to be expected, but should not put him off in any way.

"Kenneth Buttenshaw then joined us and took me off to his spacious study overlooking the expansive grounds of the property, beyond which I could see the roofline and chimneys of his factory. For some time he talked about the nature of his business. He had started his small weaving enterprise twenty years earlier, but had really seen it flourish as a result of his expansion into the production of Coburg cloth, which he explained was piece-dyed twill dress fabric. The key to his success appears to have been the employment of a young chemist, by the name of Callum Ford, who has pioneered a new process for dyeing the factory's cloth since joining the business some five years ago. They are now selling their cloth in all parts of the Empire.

"I said to Mr. Buttenshaw that the school was very happy to accept the admission of Simon into Harrow, but would need him to sign the various papers I had brought with me. Buttenshaw said he did not have his glasses to hand and indicated that he would be unable to sign any papers without them. However, with a tug on a bell cord near the desk of the study, he suggested that could be easily remedied. Moments later a slim, fresh-faced young woman with tied-back blond hair entered the study and gave me a most radiant smile. Buttenshaw introduced me to his daughter, saying that she organised all of his secretarial and administrative affairs. Sophia took charge, reading carefully through each document and then signing all of the relevant sections.

"Having completed the formalities, I was then invited to join the family for a light luncheon, although Buttenshaw gave his apologies about half an hour later, explaining that he had to go down to the factory, as there had been an unexpected problem with one of the steam-driven looms used in the production process. Simon then excused himself, saying that he had planned to do a spot of fishing in the trout steam bordering their land. That left me in the company of Sophia for the better part of three hours, chatting comfortably about our respective pasts and interests, our hopes and aspirations. It was clear that we both felt the attraction and when it came for me to leave she shook my hand tenderly and held my gaze, asking me first to take good care of her brother at Harrow and then specifically asking for me to write to her on a regular basis and to visit again soon to keep her informed of his progress. We both knew that it was a signal of affection.

"I have since then continued to write to Sophia and have made the journey to Darlington five times. The lady herself has also visited the school twice, checking on her brother, but equally spending time with me. Three weeks ago, she attended a business meeting with a law firm in town, took a room at the *Clarendon* in Bond Street and accepted my invitation to dine at *Bertolini's* in the West End and to take in a show. That evening we talked about a possible engagement. This would have been no great surprise to Simon, who had mentioned more than once his sister's growing attachment to me, but I was not so sure how her father might react. As a result, I took the decision to write to Kenneth Buttenshaw, declaring my intentions and asking for his blessing on the betrothal. Two days later, I received a decidedly lukewarm response from the man which stated that Sophia was far too young to marry and would, in all likelihood, prefer to wed someone with greater prospects than my own. As if that were not damning enough, the following day I received a letter from Sophia herself. She declared that she was deeply upset that I should have taken matters into my own hands and written to her father in such a way and asked that I desist from entering into any further communications with her. And that is how the matter now stands."

Holmes raised an eyebrow and smiled gently. "How has Simon Buttenshaw reacted to this news?"

I could only be honest with him. "Not well, I'm afraid. He has been tearful at the revelations and says that he has no idea why his sister and father have reacted so unfavourably towards me. His own letters to Sophia have brought no change of heart and he is too terrified to speak to his father of the matter for fear of upsetting the man. The last thing he wants is to be removed from Harrow, where he feels he is making such good progress."

"I see. And do you by any chance have the two letters on you, Mr. Hughes?"

Cedric shuffled uncomfortably beside me. He knew that I had carried the letters around with me since first receiving them. I had continually re-read them and talked to him about their contents, desperate to know if anything could be done to rectify the situation. As a loyal friend, he had advised me to let the matter rest and to get on with my life. His insistence that I join our friends for a day at the races was the first step in that direction. I withdrew the letters from an inside pocket of my jacket and passed them to Holmes. The look on his face suggested that he already knew I would have them with me.

He spent some time examining the two envelopes using a magnifying glass which he retrieved from a pocket of his waistcoat and made a point of smelling the paper. He then unfurled the contents of both letters and examined each in a meticulous fashion. It was a good five minutes before he ventured any comment.

"Fascinating, Mr Hughes – and most revealing. The second letter is clearly from Sophia Buttenshaw. There is no mistaking the feminine flourish of the hand and you may have observed that the paper carries with it more than a hint of Creed scent, a choice perfume which is also favoured by our dear Queen."

"That is certainly the scent Sophia uses, Mr. Holmes. But why is that significant?" I enquired.

"Well, it seems odd that a young woman writing to you in such definitive terms about the ending of a relationship should still think to add a touch of scent to the note. I would suggest that it betrays her mixed emotions," he replied.

"Then there is still a chance for me," I spluttered, eagerly clinging on to any hope of reconciliation.

"That remains to be seen," was all that Holmes had to offer. "As for the first letter, I have serious doubts about its penmanship. Kenneth Buttenshaw has not written this. The key question is whether he dictated it or had any knowledge of its contents."

Cedric was every bit as stunned as I was. "You think the letter is a forgery, then?"

Holmes scanned the document once more before replying. "There is certainly deception at work here, gentlemen. The strong hand and clipped phraseology suggest a writer some years younger than Buttenshaw. It seems clear from your earlier account, Mr. Hughes, that the factory owner cannot in fact read or write. That is why he pulled the ruse of suggesting that he could not sign his son's school admission papers without his glasses and called for Sophia's assistance. And yet, he did not ask for his glasses, but allowed her to both read all of the papers and then sign them. That she did not ask for his consent or disclose the nature of what she had just signed, demonstrated that this was a familiar practice."

I was mystified. "So, are you suggesting that Sophia also wrote the first letter?"

Holmes was adamant. "No. The two notes are in completely different hands. This letter was written by a man. He is left-handed, of slender build and an American by birth. More significantly, he is an accomplished scientist."

I could not help but laugh out loud at the apparent absurdity of what he had just revealed. "Mr. Holmes, I have no wish to be ungrateful or discourteous to you, but are you really asking us to believe that you can discern all of that from a cursory glance at a handwritten letter?"

I feared that I had insulted the fellow, but Holmes responded with admirable composure: "My methods are unusual, but the results speak for themselves. It is really a process of research, observation and evaluation, linking all of the available facts. The wording of the letter is short, direct and offhand. There is no hint of sentiment or feeling, strongly suggesting a male hand. The almost imperceptible thumbprint on the front of the document and the two finger impressions to the rear, demonstrate that the hands of the author are long and slender. I would expect his general frame to be similar. That he is left-handed is evident from the way that the ink has been smudged in parts as his writing hand moves across the page. And the deposit along the bottom edge of the document suggests that he had recent close contact with coal tar, a chemical used in the process of dyeing cloth."

Cedric and I were both astounded, but a nagging doubt still remained in my mind. "I can see the logic of all that you have revealed so far, but what about his place of birth?"

"A strong suggestion from the word '*gotten*' which you will note in the second paragraph. However, to understand fully why I believe he is not a native of this country, we must turn to the nature of Miss Buttenshaw's business meeting in London a few weeks back."

"Really?" I retorted, staggered that the matter should have any particular relevance to the letter.

"Yes," said Holmes. "Do you remember the date that the meeting took place and which particular legal firm Sophia visited?"

I thought hard for a few seconds before responding. "Monday, 17th May – I remember, because it was the day after my mother's birthday. As for the law firm, I believe their name was Dennington & Fanshawe."

There was no disguising his delight. "Excellent! Then my working hypothesis seems to be solid enough. I should explain, gentlemen, that a major component of my investigative approach is the study of chemistry. I use the science to uncover some of the unseen human traces and concealed clues that others may miss. As such, I pay particular attention to any developments within the scientific field. Dennington & Fanshawe are a very prominent firm of patent lawyers. About a month ago, there was a small piece in the legal section of *The Times* announcing that the firm is acting for a chemist who has taken out a patent on a new process for dyeing cloth, which uses a compound of coal tar and other chemical elements."

Cedric could immediately see the likely relevance. "And you believe that this has some connection to the Buttenshaw factory?"

Holmes nodded and brought his hands together. "Without doubt, you see the chemist who secured the patent was a twenty-seven year old Texan... by the name of Callum Ford."

My surprise at the disclosure was palpable, although I could not immediately see what relevance it had to the letter. Holmes then continued: "Buttenshaw told you that he employed the man some five years ago. The young chemist must have come with some considerable reputation or expertise to convince the industrialist to engage his services. But the faith or trust of the older man clearly paid off. With the new dyeing process, the business has gone from strength to strength. So, how did Ford view this rapid expansion?

Perhaps he felt that he should benefit from a greater share of the wealth being created."

I ventured a quick comment. "Mr. Holmes, I did not meet the chemist on any of my visits to Darlington, but both Kenneth and Sophia had mentioned that he had been placed in a position of some responsibility and left to run much of the manufactory single-handedly. From their comments, I had always taken it that they believed him to be more than adequately remunerated for his role. I suspect there may also have been some friction between Ford and Sophia, however, as she admitted to me once that she disliked him coming up to the house and lingering in her father's study, which he was inclined to do whenever Kenneth was away on business."

Holmes listened assiduously before commenting. "That is a very significant piece of information. It suggests that the household staff would be used to seeing Mr. Ford at the house and, in his position, the American clearly felt that he was at liberty to deputise for his employer. Let us suppose, then, that he was in Kenneth Buttenshaw's study when your letter arrived. It is not so far-fetched to imagine him opening the correspondence, as I am sure that he also knew of Buttenshaw's inability to read and write. And having read the correspondence, he then writes back to you purporting to be his employer. So, do we think he did this with Buttenshaw's blessing?"

Cedric and I answered in unison, "No." Feeling some relief at the suggestion that the letter had not come directly from Buttenshaw, I then added, "Kenneth may have been concerned about Sophia marrying, but I know the man well enough to believe that he would have told me face to face if he had any particular reservations about me personally. He cannot have failed to observe how close the two of us have become in recent months."

Holmes continued. "If we take that as an accurate assessment, what possible motive would Ford have had for falsifying the letter?"

Cedric offered a suggestion. "Perhaps he believed that if Sophia married and were taken away from Darlington, the business might suffer, with Kenneth Buttenshaw unable to deal with all of the administrative affairs of the factory."

"I think that unlikely, Mr. Stone. In fact, if Callum Ford had desires to take a more controlling role within the business, such a development would have played right into his hands. With Sophia out of the way, Buttenshaw would have little choice but to relinquish even more power to the chemist."

"Then you do believe that Ford's ultimate plan was to wrest ownership of the business away from Buttenshaw?" I then asked.

"Yes." Holmes paused briefly, removing a small briar pipe from a pocket which he proceeded to fill from a leather pouch. "Applying for and securing an industrial patent can take some time. I have little doubt that Ford registered the patent application as soon as he realised the new dyeing process worked effectively. And now that he has successfully obtained the patent, he could hold the factory to ransom. Without the dyeing process, Buttenshaw will be unable to continue to manufacture his lucrative Coburg cloth."

A brass band struck up somewhere in the distance. In the late afternoon there was still a lot of activity across the fair, although I barely registered any of it, so intent was I on listening to what Holmes had to say. He continued to expound on his thoughts. "Kenneth Buttenshaw must now know of Ford's successful patent application, but he may not have realised the full ramifications of it."

It was Cedric who then interjected. "Why do you say that?"

"I believe there is a more logical explanation for what has occurred and the intentions that Callum Ford now has," reasoned Holmes. "Let us suppose that his primary reason for intercepting and responding to the letter from Mr. Hughes was to stop the engagement happening. He pens his response and then tells Miss Buttenshaw what he has done, revealing his own affections for her."

I choked at the suggestion, trying to stifle my anger. "Sophia would hear none of it! She would not be swayed by such a man. It is unthinkable, Mr. Holmes!"

"Not if he then threatened to ruin the business by taking his services and ownership of the patent with him. After her meeting with the patent lawyers, she would be fully aware of the position that Ford now occupied, news that she may well have kept from her father in trying to protect him. At the very least, I believe that Ford forced her to write to you, ending the courtship – a task she appears to have done with a very heavy heart. But he may still entertain the notion that he can win her affections and take over the business. A convenient marriage would enable him to achieve both."

Cedric could see my obvious distress and intervened. "How much of this is likely to be known by Kenneth Buttenshaw?" he asked.

"I would say that he knows nothing of what has occurred," came the reply. "If he is as direct and resourceful as you have suggested, Mr. Hughes, I imagine he would not take too kindly to anyone trying to blackmail one of his children."

I regained my composure on hearing this. "I will not give up on this matter. How do you think I should now proceed?"

As with all of the revelations he had imparted that afternoon, his response was not what I had expected: "You must leave this affair in my capable hands. I cannot promise to resolve it overnight, but would hope to bring you some news within a few days." And with that, he would speak no more of the matter. Some twenty minutes later he thanked us for our hospitality and with a broad smile and swift wave of the hand left the fair to head back to London.

Two days passed, and on the morning of the third day he was as good as his word. I received a knock on the door of my private study just before ten o'clock. A young pupil handed me a telegram which had just been delivered. The message was short and blunt. Holmes would be visiting the school that afternoon with news – I was to expect him at three o'clock.

The arrival of the Clarence carriage that afternoon created quite a stir, the clatter of the growler's wheels, and clip-clopping of the horses' hooves on the fan-laid cobbles along the approach to the school, turning many a head. I raced from the refectory to greet the carriage and was taken aback to see that Holmes was not alone. Accompanying him were Kenneth Buttenshaw and my dear Sophia. Kenneth was effusive in his greeting, removing his Derby, shaking my hand vigorously and announcing how good it was to see me. Sophia held my gaze – just as she had the first time we met - and then stepped down from the carriage as I steadied her left arm. She too removed her hat and then moved forward to kiss me lightly on the cheek. I knew instantly that Holmes had managed to bring some resolution to the case and beamed at my beloved, forgetting momentarily that the scene was being played out under the gaze of a hundred or more schoolboys.

When we reached my study, I promptly despatched one of the prefects to arrange for Simon to be brought to the room to see his father and sister and then ordered some extra tea cups, scones and jam to accompany those that I had already laid out for Holmes. The man himself was immaculately turned out in a top hat, blue-black morning jacket and waistcoat, sharply pressed trousers, keenly starched dress shirt and green silk bow tie. When we were all seated he began to explain all that had been achieved.

"Mr. Hughes, you will forgive my somewhat furtive approach in asking the Buttenshaws to accompany me here this afternoon. This morning we attended a meeting at the offices of Dennington & Fanshawe where we successfully negotiated a deal with Callum Ford for the continued use of his patented dyeing process at the Darlington factory. In return for a twenty-five percent share of all future net profits, Mr. Ford has agreed to return to his home city of San Antonio in Texas and to cease to have any further involvement in the business. He has already instructed another young chemist to take over his duties. I am sure that Mr. Buttenshaw can speak for himself, but I believe this outcome to be the best for all parties concerned."

Buttenshaw seemed pleased to echo Holmes's words. "When Sophia returned from her trip to London a month ago and told me all about the patent situation, I thought that we were done for. But Callum said not a word to me. I had no idea that he had falsified the letter to you, Mr. Hughes, and certainly had no inkling that he had any intentions towards my dear daughter. I need hardly say that I would have risked bankruptcy, imprisonment or even death rather than allow him to take my daughter's hand without her consent, and I would have seen myself destitute before I would have agreed to his takeover of my business. I will be forever grateful to you for inviting Mr. Holmes to assist us – he has been an invaluable ally in bringing all of this to my attention and steering us down the path of reconciliation. Now, having said my piece, I believe that Sophia also has something to tell you..."

Sophia looked momentarily forlorn before a thin smile lit up her delicate features. "I fear I have treated you despicably, Geraint, despite all of the warmth and affection you have shown to me and my family. Callum told me how he had intercepted your letter to my father and contrived a response. I did not know how to counter his threats and intimidation in protecting myself, my father and the business. I reluctantly agreed to write to you, in the way that I did, on the basis that Callum allow me six months to think about his proposal of marriage. I could see no other recourse at the time, but realise now that I should have trusted my instincts and confided in both you and my father in exposing Callum for the scoundrel he really is."

I leaned across and squeezed her hand. "Nothing further needs to be said, but there is still one outstanding matter which has yet to be determined."

She looked up anxiously as a tear rolled down her cheek. "And what is that?" she queried, her hand reaching for a small pocket handkerchief within her sleeve.

"Why, the date of our wedding, my dear. With your father's blessing, we have still to arrange the time and place of our marriage!"

There was considerable humour and much banter in the moments that followed and it was with some reluctance that my soon to be father-in-law announced a short time thereafter that they must return to the carriage for the ride back to King's Cross and the train journey home to County Durham. Having arranged for Kenneth and Sophia to be escorted back to their waiting carriage after saying farewell to Simon, I took the opportunity to speak directly to Holmes before he too headed off to town. "Mr. Holmes, I stand in awe of your remarkable talents and will always be in your debt for the way that you have assisted me. And yet, I feel certain that there is something in this case that you have been reluctant to reveal. I fail to see why Callum Ford, with all of the cards stacked in his favour, should have agreed to your proposals so readily."

There was a look of uneasiness and perhaps a hint of frustration in the way that he met my gaze and then responded to the challenge. "There is no point in misleading you, Mr. Hughes. I would not want this to become common knowledge, but – to continue with your own analogy – I did indeed have a trump card to play. My older brother, Mycroft, occupies a position of some seniority within the British Civil Service and works hard to maintain a close cohort of personal contacts within the Foreign and Commonwealth Office. A word in his ear was sufficient to prompt a visit to Darlington by a high-ranking official from the American Embassy in London. Ford was told to accept the offer that was put to him; a deal that will, in all likelihood, make him an extremely rich man. He understood that any failure to acquiesce would result in his immediate detention and eventual expulsion from this country on a charge of espionage – high-handed perhaps, but the only way to secure his silence and compliance in this delicate matter."

"I see," was all that I could think to say, feeling somewhat unnerved by the disclosure and realising clearly that Holmes operated in a frighteningly different world from that which I enjoyed at Harrow. I shook his hand a final time and walked him out to the waiting carriage.

It was at that moment that I realised I had forgotten to ask him about his fees on the case. Rather indelicately, I put the question to him as the door to the carriage was swung open by a beaming Kenneth Buttenshaw. To my astonishment, the industrialist took it upon himself to answer for Holmes: "There is no need to worry about that, young man. Mr. Holmes and I have reached a very satisfactory settlement and I have indicated that if he is ever in any financial need, he has only to approach me. You have a lot to learn about business that this fine school can never teach you." He winked at Sophia. "Luckily, you are marrying a woman who can find her way around a balance sheet and knows all about profit and loss."

The four of us laughed and Holmes turned to me a final time before climbing into the carriage. "Farewell, Mr. Hughes. I wish all of my cases had such satisfying conclusions. At this stage, I have to be honest in saying that I am not sure whether my chosen career will continue to be such a success."

I was cheered by his frank admission and responded without hesitation. "You need have no doubts on that score. You have a rare combination of talents and abilities that clearly set you apart from other men. The world awaits your arrival."

I waved them off and lingered awhile as the carriage disappeared from view. I knew then that it would not be the last time that I would hear of Mr. Sherlock Holmes.

2. The Fashionably Dressed Girl

Those of you who have a mind for these things might well remember that in *A Study in Scarlet* I recorded some of the early visitors to our Baker Street apartment in the days before I appreciated fully the nature of my friend's singular occupation. In a rather dismissive fashion, I wrote that: '*One morning a young girl called, fashionably dressed, and stayed for half an hour or more.*' It was Holmes himself who pointed out, sometime afterwards – when he had first read what he referred to as my "amusingly anecdotal" account of our earliest adventure together – that the young woman I had seen that day was later to feature in another of his cases. To that point, I had been wholly unaware that when Miss Madelaine Fremont called at 221B one afternoon in the November of 1881, it was not the first time she had entered the upstairs consulting room.

Holmes later explained that her first visit had been a trifling affair about a family inheritance which he had been able to sort out with very little effort. The case I now set before you was an entirely different matter.

With her cape and hat removed, I could see that the young woman was a little over five feet in height, slim, graceful and pretty. Her small oval-shaped face was framed with a high crown of auburn hair in the style of a French twist, with a loose fringe across her delicate forehead. In her early-twenties, she was quite the society lady; her blue crinoline fan skirt was narrow-fitting with a long bodice extending down to her tiny waist. I had rarely seen a more engaging and fashionable girl.

Holmes seemed oblivious to her charms and with a thin smile, terse greeting and single wave of his hand, directed her towards the seat nearest the fire. She seemed unperturbed, sitting most elegantly and taking time to remove her long blue gloves which she placed deftly on the arm of the chair. My colleague took it upon himself to lead the introductions. "My dear Miss Fremont, this gentleman is my colleague, Dr. Watson, with whom I share this apartment. Watson has recently been assisting with a number of my cases, so you may trust his discretion on any matter you wish to bring to my attention."

She nodded and responded in a clear, confident voice, with just the hint of a foreign accent. "Thank you, Mr. Holmes. That is understood. And I am very pleased to make your acquaintance, Dr. Watson. My name is Madelaine Fremont." I thanked her quickly, allowing her to carry on. "I am a woman of independent means and make a comfortable living assisting a number of wealthy ladies in matters of style and taste. In short, I help them to choose the most appropriate items for their wardrobe."

My surprise at the nature of her vocation must have been evident for she felt it necessary to explain further: "While my father was English and I grew up in Oxford, my late mother, Genevieve, came from the province of Lorraine in the north-eastern corner of France. She was an accomplished dressmaker and when I was fourteen encouraged me to train as a seamstress. I was fortunate in securing a position working for the couturier Charles Frederick Worth in his prestigious Parisian fashion house on the Rue de la Paix. My mother was so proud, but sadly died before I could complete my apprenticeship..."

She paused at this point and I could see that the mention of her mother had clearly moved her. Regaining her composure, she then added: "Two years ago, my father also passed away and - after some family difficulties – I was left with a modest inheritance..." She cast a quick glance towards Holmes, although my colleague displayed no reaction. "...Monsieur Worth was very understanding when I announced that I would be leaving his employment. Since that time, I have used my knowledge of fashion to guide my wealthy patrons and have introduced many British and American women to the delights of Parisian *haute couture*."

I was slightly bewildered as to where this was all heading but felt it polite to respond. "I see. Well, I cannot claim to know much about dress-making, but your name intrigues me. You said your father was English, but the name 'Fremont' has a distinct Gallic ring to it."

She nodded. "Yes, it was my mother's maiden name, deriving, I believe, from the village of *Framont* in Lorraine, close to where my forebears lived. My given surname was 'Strathclyde', but when I began working in Paris, I thought the name 'Madelaine Fremont' would be more acceptable to my Continental colleagues. I have been known by that name ever since."

Holmes then interjected somewhat brusquely. "Miss Fremont, your earlier telegram mentioned something about a strange visit that you had couple of days ago and some fears you have about your safety. Perhaps you can enlighten us as to the basic facts and sequence of events?"

Our client seemed to take no offence at my colleague's directness. She sat forward in the chair and addressed him. "Certainly, Mr. Holmes. I appreciate that you are not one for blather. As you know, since moving to London, I have rented a very pleasant house on Upper Brook Street. It has proved to be an ideal location for my work – close to the fashionable

31

heart of Mayfair and providing me with sufficient space to store my extensive collection of dresses and fabric samples. I arrange appointments with my ladies and they visit my home to choose outfits which suit them. Two days ago, on the Tuesday, a couple called on me at the address. They introduced themselves as 'Mr. and Mrs. Reynolds'."

"And had they made a prior appointment?" asked Holmes quickly.

"No. It struck me as being unusual at the time. So far so, that my first question to the woman was how she knew of me. For I have nothing on the front of the building to advertise my business, which is all conducted by word of mouth. She said that '...a friend of a friend' had once used my services and I therefore came 'highly recommended.' I was at once flattered and invited them in to the house.

"In order to properly display all of my dresses and other items, I have given over the sizeable front parlour and a further adjoining room to the business. The parlour is used for the initial consultation with my clients, who are then invited through to the back room to browse my collection. While seated in the parlour with the Reynolds, I asked my young assistant, Abigail, to bring us a pot of fresh tea and then began to ask Mrs. Reynolds how I could assist her. But then a strange thing happened..."

"Which was?"

"Mrs. Reynolds had to this point been carrying a most remarkable cat in a small wicker basket. It was a chocolate-brown colour, with a delicate triangular face, pointed ears and light-blue almond-shaped eyes. She explained that it was a rare female Siamese cat. With no warning whatsoever, the animal started to make the most hideous wailing sound and began to scramble to get out of the basket. At one point it scratched Mrs. Reynolds on the hand, drawing blood, and, having exited the basket, proceeded to run around the parlour in a desperate attempt to evade capture. As it did so, two small silver bells on its collar rang melodically, making the whole scene rather comical. This carried on for some minutes until Abigail entered the room carrying the tea tray and provided the cat with an escape route. Mrs. Reynolds screamed uncontrollably and said the pet must not be allowed to get away as it was, 'an extremely valuable housecat'."

I had imagined that Holmes might be disinterested in this feline caper, but he was listening intently to every word.

"We chased the cat as it made its way through the downstairs rooms and through to the kitchen at the back of the house. With the kitchen door ajar, the Siamese ran at speed out into the back garden. Mrs. Reynolds screamed once more and directed her husband to go after it. I tried to explain to her that my high-walled garden would easily contain the cat. And so it was, that five minutes later, I was able to coax the petrified pet from beneath a box hedge.

"We made our way back to the parlour and resumed our discussions, but the cat would not be parted from me and hissed every time the Reynolds approached her. I have always had an affinity with cats and the animal warmed to me. The pair seemed content just to have the Siamese back and Mrs. Reynolds began to explain what it was she wanted. In short, she had a very specific green dress in mind – one that had been launched in Paris that very summer. She had even brought with her an advertisement for the dress that had appeared in *The Queen* magazine. She asked whether it would be possible to obtain a dress similar to that advertised, for much less than the cost of the original, in a short space of time. I explained that it was indeed possible, as most *couture* is immediately copied by less prestigious dressmakers and sold at more affordable prices - I needed only to take her measurements and could have a dress ready within a couple of days. Mrs. Reynolds was delighted and said that she would return for the dress on Friday. I then took her measurements and wrote out a receipt for the deposit she paid on the dress, before seeing the couple to the door."

"And what did Mr. Reynolds do while all of this was taking place?" I asked, imagining the poor fellow to have been like a fish out of water.

I received a coquettish grin from our guest. "Like most men, he had little to say about his wife's choice of dress. For the most part he sat quietly, nodding occasionally and agreeing with everything she said. I took Mrs. Reynold's measurements in the back room, leaving him in the parlour. When we returned, he had somehow managed to get the cat back into the basket, although it did not look happy with the arrangement at all. The couple then left, hailing the first hansom that passed by."

Holmes reached for his churchman and began to fill the bowl with a pinch of tobacco. "What were your immediate thoughts when the couple first left, Miss Fremont?"

"I had the distinct impression that the cat did not belong to the couple, Mr. Holmes."

"I see. Anything else?"

"Yes. While they were reasonably well-dressed, their attire did not suggest that they were particularly wealthy. Mrs. Reynolds' outfit was drab and inexpensive, a distinct contrast to the dress she wished to purchase. When the Siamese was sat on my lap, I could not help but notice the leather collar around its neck. In addition to the two silver bells, there was a small gold locket beneath the cat's throat and the collar was studded with diamonds."

Holmes looked up sharply. "Diamonds, you say? *Real* diamonds?"

"Without a doubt. Working with the many fashionable ladies that I do, I know a real diamond when I see one. And these were diamonds of the very best quality. It also seemed odd, if the pet were 'an extremely valuable housecat', that the couple should carry it around in such a cheap wicker basket. Altogether, I was left with the uneasy feeling that something was not quite right. And yet, Mrs. Reynolds happily paid the one-third deposit for the dress and seemed eager to return for it later in the week."

"Yes indeed. But why is it that you now fear for your safety? Has something else happened?"

Miss Fremont's demeanour changed and she began to look more solemn. "Yes, Mr. Holmes. Again, it was all very odd. Abigail works with me until about five o'clock each day. Beyond that, I live alone. I suppose it must have been about nine o'clock that evening when I retired. I had something of a headache and decided to have an early night. My bedroom is at the front of the house. It was quiet at that time, and as I lay in bed I thought I could hear the jingle of bells out in the street. Instantly, I was reminded of the Siamese. And as I listened, thought I heard a cat meow. I got out of bed and walked to the window. I could not see below the porch of the door, but again heard a cat. Intrigued, I wrapped my dressing gown around me and went down to the front door. When I opened it, a cat ran in and began to rub against my ankles. From the lamplight in the street I could see that it was indeed the Siamese cat with the ornate collar."

I was intrigued by her account and, like Holmes, keen to hear what had happened after that. Miss Fremont continued in her confident tone.

"The poor cat seemed hungry and eagerly consumed some chicken I had in the pantry. She was content to follow me upstairs as I returned to my room and slept soundly on the bed at my feet for the rest of the night. So when I awoke yesterday morning, I had to decide what to do. Somewhat against my better judgement, I determined that I ought to try and find where Mr. and Mrs. Reynolds lived, so as to return the cat to them. In the event, I thought the task would be easy, for on the underside of the cat's collar was stamped an address in Piccadilly."

Holmes was relishing the narrative. "No doubt the address of the cat's real owner. So what happened next?"

"I took a cab and travelled the short distance from Upper Brook Street to Sutherland House, a grand property close to Devonshire House. I knew before I arrived at the front entrance that this was unlikely to be the home of the Reynolds. A smartly tailored butler answered the door and was delighted to see the Siamese. I explained how I had found the cat and had taken it in for the night, but deliberately did not mention the Reynolds. The butler said that his mistress would be overjoyed and invited me to step in off the street. The lady of the house was a Mrs. Sarah Van Allen. She was elated at seeing the cat and could not thank me enough for finding and returning her beloved pet. While she was expressing her gratitude, I noticed that she paid particular attention to the locket around the cat's neck. I had not thought to check it myself, but watched as she opened it quickly and glanced inside. In that brief moment, I saw that it contained a small key and noted also that Mrs. Van Allen appeared to be very visibly relieved, having checked this."

"Capital! Your observational skills do you credit. I believe we are beginning to get to the bottom of this mystery."

"Yes. But I have not yet told you the most remarkable feature of my encounter with Mrs. Van Allen."

Holmes beamed. "I really do not wish to steal your thunder, Miss Fremont, but was she wearing a distinctive and fashionable green dress, just like the one that Mrs. Reynolds wished to procure?"

Our client looked astonished. "How could you possibly know that?"

"It was really the only solution which would fit the facts as we know them. There is a criminal endeavour at the centre of this, I am convinced of that. And I take it that your security fears are based around the fact that you now know the Reynolds to be charlatans of some kind."

She nodded reluctantly. "That is exactly my fear. I am terrified that they will arrive tomorrow for the dress and have some ulterior motive for wanting to gain entry to my house for a second time. I implore you to help me, Mr. Holmes."

I knew already that my colleague had no intention of letting the matter rest there. And I was equally clear that I would do everything I could to protect this remarkable young woman. Holmes gave her an assurance that he would look into the case further and promised that both of us would be at Upper Brook Street when the Reynolds arrived the following morning at ten o'clock.

Miss Fremont left us a short while later. I escorted her to the door and hailed a cab for her outside 221B. When I had climbed back up the seventeen steps to our apartment, I saw that Holmes had donned a thick overcoat and deerstalker hat and had a walking cane to hand. At my polite enquiry, he announced that he had a couple of errands to attend to, but would be back for supper. In the short time that I had known him, I already recognised that Holmes sometimes preferred to work on his own and at his own pace.

****

It was close to eight o'clock that evening when I heard him return. Mrs. Hudson had prepared a large shepherd's pie for our supper and was placing it on the table of the study. She seemed relieved that my colleague had arrived back at just the right time.

"Mrs. Hudson! Your timing is impeccable. I am ravenous! And I think Dr. Watson and I will enjoy a bottle of *Beaujolais nouveau* with our meal. I have just received twelve bottles from a grateful French client, so we ought to sample its delights!"

We both tucked in to the hearty faire and Holmes explained the nature of his earlier enquiries. "I paid a short visit to Mrs. Sarah Van Allen. An extremely genial lady who was most concerned to hear that a scheme had been hatched to dispossess her of the Siamese cat. When I explained that the thieves had sought only to obtain the key secreted within the gold locket, she was astounded. With what she had to tell me, I now have a clear outline of the crime being planned by the Reynolds."

"Which is?"

"Grand larceny. Mrs. Van Allen's husband spends most of the year working in the Dutch East Indies. He trades in tea and silk mainly, but is also something of a gem collector. Each month he sends his wife a parcel containing one or two precious stones. Fearful of leaving these in Sutherland House, Mrs. Van Allen makes a monthly trip to Coutts & Co. in The

Strand. Here she has a large safe deposit box into which she deposits the gemstones..."

"...and the key that opens the box is kept in the gold locket around the cat's neck!"

"Exactly! Our would-be thieves took the cat on Tuesday and had a fresh key cut to match the original. They then hoped to return the animal to Sutherland House before its absence had been noted."

"A task that they clearly botched. But how did you know they had a duplicate key made?"

"Before visiting Mrs. Van Allen I called in at the cab depot closest to Upper Brook Street. I took a punt, but figured that the driver who had picked up the Reynolds outside Miss Fremont's may have been locally based. It was a gamble that paid off. I tracked down the very helpful Mr. Trimble, who clearly remembered the couple, *and the cat*. He explained that they set off, having asked to be dropped off at an address in Pimlico. The hansom had not travelled more than a couple of hundred yards, when the cabbie heard a frantic knocking from inside. He pulled over only to see a brown cat leap from the cab and sprint off down the street. With no hope of catching the animal, his exasperated passengers had asked him to carry on towards their destination."

I laughed at the humour of it all. "So that explains how the cat was still in Upper Brook Street when Miss Fremont took it in."

"Yes. Now the couple alighted from the cab at the *Marquis of Westminster* public house. I went there myself and discovered that there is a locksmith close-by. Having knocked at the door of his premises for some minutes, the proprietor answered, and – with the inducement of a few shillings –

recollected that a couple had called earlier in that day, requesting that a duplicate key be cut from the one they presented. He said the woman had been carrying a wicker basket in which was a sleeping cat. In fact, the Siamese looked to be sleeping so soundly that the locksmith wondered if the cat was actually dead!"

"Very suggestive, Holmes. Do you think it had been drugged?"

"Most likely. It would explain how they were able to take the cat in the first place without raising any alarm in the house."

We finished what remained of the pie and downed another glass of the excellent *Beaujolais*. I was still unclear on a number of points and continued to ask questions. "Surely the Reynolds cannot hope to carry on with their plan? Having lost the cat, does that not give the game away?"

"Not necessarily," replied Holmes. "They still have the duplicate key. And until I alerted Mrs. Van Allen, she had no inkling that anyone might plot to steal the original key. You see she was under the impression that only she knew of its hiding place."

"Ah, ha! Then if the Siamese is a house cat that can only mean one thing..."

"...that one of the household staff is implicated – my thoughts exactly, Watson. Mrs. Van Allen has a butler, an under-butler, a housekeeper, two maids and a carriage driver. In the short time I was at Sutherland House I was unable to speak to any of the staff, but have my suspicions. I hope to put my theory to the test tomorrow, when hopefully we will get the chance to meet the Reynolds."

Before turning in for the night, I had one final query. "I understand that they have a key for the safe deposit box, but how do they expect to walk into a reputable bank like Coutts & Co. and be given access to the vault? Mrs. Van Allen is likely to be a recognisable figure given her frequent trips and the bank prides itself on its very personal service."

Holmes nodded and grinned widely. "I believe that is where the newly commissioned green dress comes in to its own. Coats, hats, scarves and gloves are relatively easy to obtain, but an expensive piece of Parisian fashion is a different matter. A discerning manager will have an eye for such things in a bank like Coutts & Co.!"

****

I slept fitfully that night, turning over all of the facts of the case and trying to imagine what would happen the following morning. I woke a little after six o'clock and was shaved, washed, dressed and breakfasted before Holmes stirred.

We set off in good time. It was another cold, yet sunny, day and Holmes insisted on walking the mile and a half to Upper Brook Street. Miss Freemont was overjoyed to see us and looked every bit as radiant as she had the previous day. We were introduced to her assistant, Abigail, and Holmes then explained what would happen. Abigail would greet the couple at the door and show them into the front parlour. Miss Freemont would then enter and explain that she had been unable to obtain the dress and would return the Reynolds' deposit to them. This would be the signal for Holmes and me to enter the room and confront the pair. Until that point, we would be hidden away in the front room opposite the parlour.

Our couple arrived a few minutes before their appointed time. Standing behind the net curtains of the front room, Holmes and I had an opportunity to study them as they stepped down from a cab and walked up to the door. The man was a little over six feet in height, strongly built and clean-shaven. The woman at his side was also tall, elegant in her features, yet plainly clothed. Both looked to be in their mid-thirties.

The plan worked like clockwork. And it was quite clear that until Holmes and I barged our way into the parlour, the Reynolds had no idea that their underhanded scheme had been exposed. On seeing us, it was the man who immediately turned defensive: "Who are you? What is it you want from us?"

Holmes came straight to the point. "I think it is more a question of what you wanted from Mrs. Van Allen, Mr. Beerton."

The use of his real name had clearly shocked the man. He looked as if he were about to say something further, but could not seem to articulate the words. The woman beside him then spoke. "I think we're done for – these gentlemen must be the police."

"We are not the police, Madam," replied Holmes, "but will be accompanying you to the nearest police station in a short while. We just need some further information from you to complete our investigation into your scheme to rob Mrs. Van Allen's safe deposit box."

Beerton had clearly found his voice again and rose from his seat to confront Holmes. "How do you know who I am? In fact, how do you know any of this?"

Holmes stood face to face with Beerton. "Sit down, Sir. My name is Sherlock Holmes and I am a consulting detective. This is my colleague, Dr. Watson. You have nothing to gain by offering violence."

Beerton looked from Holmes towards me and then sat back down. Holmes then continued.

"I have neither the time nor the inclination to provide you with the full details of *how* we uncovered your plot to rob Mrs. Van Allen. But I will tell you *what* I know. Firstly, your name is Andrew Beerton and you work as a groom and carriage driver for the Van Allen family, a post you have held for the past five years. Each month, Mrs. Van Allen takes a trip to Coutts & Co. on The Strand. Here she deposits the precious gems that her husband sends her from overseas. It is your job to drive the carriage and to then accompany Mrs. Van Allen into the bank, nominally ensuring her safety as she carries with her a bag containing the valuables.

"In this role, you observed a pattern. Mrs. Van Allen enters the lobby, walks to the reception area and then asks to see one of the bank's managers. She is greeted by one of four managers each time. They exchange a few pleasantries and he accompanies her to the locked door of the vault in which the safe deposit boxes are held. Here he leaves Mrs. Van Allen in the capable hands of a bank employee who asks for the number of her deposit box and then, for security, requires her to produce the safe deposit key. When she does this, they unlock the heavy security door and allow her to go into the vault alone where she is able to deposit her valuables. While you are required to wait outside the vault, you know from overhearing this conversation many times that her deposit box number is 4457.

"The monthly trips to the bank are known about by all of the household staff. In fact, I imagine it is often a source of some gossip. But you found out the one piece of information that none of the others knew – namely, where Mrs. Van Allen hid the key to the safe deposit box..."

At this point, Beerton felt inclined to speak. "It was so simple. I was passing the window of her study one day and looked in to see Mrs. Van Allen stroking the cat. Unaware that I was watching, she reached for the locket and opened it. Inside I could see a small key, the same key I had watched her produce at the bank dozens of times. In that moment, I knew that with the key it would be possible to access the safe deposit box."

"But your challenge was how to get someone to pretend to be Mrs. Van Allen, someone convincing enough to fool the staff and managers at the bank. Is that when you enlisted the help of your sister here?"

It was the turn of 'Mrs. Reynolds' to look shocked. Like Beerton, she had clearly realised that there was no point in lying to my colleague. "How did you know, Mr. Holmes?"

"There is no mistaking the likeness. You are clearly siblings. And I'm certain that your name is not 'Mrs. Reynolds'."

In spite of the position that she now found herself in, the woman could only chuckle. "No, my name is Annalisa Beerton. I never married. And you must not judge my brother too harshly. It was me that put him up to it. When he told me about the key, I said it would be easy for me to assume the part of Mrs. Van Allen. She is a similar height and age to me, has the same hair colouring and an identically shaped face. For some years, I have made a rather precarious living in the theatre, so it is second nature for me to pretend to be someone else."

This time it was Madelaine Freemont who spoke. "But I suppose you realised that you needed to have a convincing costume to pull off the pretence, and that was why you approached me for the dress."

Annalisa Beerton smiled at her without any hint of malevolence. "I told Andrew it was essential. Both to convince those snooty managers at the bank that I was the well-heeled Mrs. Van Allen, but also so that I would feel appropriately dressed for the part. I had seen Mrs. Van Allen in the dress once before and knew it to be an expensive outfit. But I also knew that we could find someone to replicate it. I was not lying when I said you came highly recommended, Miss Fremont."

Our client looked somewhat embarrassed at the unexpected compliment. Annalisa Beerton then added: "Our mistake, of course, was taking that damned cat!"

Holmes could only agree with her. "Yes. I imagine that your plan was to take the Siamese for a short time, having drugged it in some way, and while the cat was comatose to arrange for a duplicate key to be cut from the original. I know that you visited a locksmith in Pimlico on your way to Miss Fremont's. Having then come here to procure the green dress, you then planned to return the cat to Sutherland House."

Andrew Beerton answered him directly. "I knew the cat was temperamental. But I was fearful of just taking the key. If Mrs. Van Allen had chanced to look in the locket and had found the key to be missing, I felt certain that she would suspect foul play. But if the cat went astray for only a few hours – and was then returned with the key – I believed that would work in our favour.

"As the groom, I have access to lots of horse treatments. I took a mild sedative and put some in the cat's food, having no real feel for how much would be needed to knock out such a small animal. It was enough to put it to sleep when I first removed the Siamese from the study, and for our trip to the locksmith's, but when we arrived here, the cat came round in a highly agitated state."

"And then you lost her altogether on the cab journey back to Pimlico..."

"Yes. At first I thought it would prove to be a disaster, but hoped that the cat would find its way home. Either way, I thought that no one would be able to guess that we had taken the Siamese and would have no clue as to our real intentions in removing it in the first place. So when I saw that the cat had indeed come back, I told Annalisa that we should continue with our plan."

Miss Freemont then interposed once more: "Did you not know that it was me who returned the cat?"

Beerton looked at her quizzically. "No, not to this point. It is less than a couple of miles from here to Piccadilly. I just assumed that the cat had made its own way back."

Holmes then continued. "Having taken the decision to continue with the robbery, were you planning to pick up the dress and then visit the bank this afternoon?"

The groom answered somewhat sheepishly. "Yes. I told Mrs. Van Allen this morning that the carriage needed some minor repairs and would need to be driven down to the blacksmith's. I expected to pick up the dress, travel back to Sutherland House and then with Annalisa suitably attired, drive the carriage to the bank. Having successfully stolen the gemstones, we believed we could return the carriage and make our escape tomorrow. I did not think that Mrs. Van Allen would realise she had been robbed until she next went to the bank. By then, Annalisa and I would have made the passage across to Holland and be living a new life abroad."

"Then I am sorry to disappoint you," said Holmes. "Watson and I have no option but to hand you over to the police for the attempted robbery. How you will fare at the hands of a judge and jury I do not know."

****

It was some weeks later when I next saw Madelaine Freemont. Holmes had asked her to call in at Baker Street for he had some news on the attempted robbery.

She was punctual in arriving just a few minutes before eleven o'clock that morning. I decided to meet her at the door and show her up. She was dressed in a deep-red velvet skirt and bustle, with a matching jacket. Her very fetching hat, parasol and slim scarlet shoes completed the overall look. I stood in admiration of her.

"How good to see you, Miss Freemont. I trust you are well?"

"Thank you, Dr. Watson. I am very well and hope the same can be said of you?"

When we entered the study, Holmes was in the process of dismantling a flintlock pistol. Miss Freemont seemed both surprised and bemused by the sight. Holmes was unperturbed: "Ah, Miss Freemont. I thought you might like to know what has happened in the case of Andrew and Annalisa Beerton. They were examined by the magistrates earlier this week on the charge of attempted robbery and have been committed to face trial at the Old Bailey next March. In all likelihood, they can expect heavy prison sentences if found guilty."

"Thank you, Mr. Holmes. I feel some sympathy for them, but I suppose the crime was very audacious."

"Yes, they were foolhardy in their endeavour. But the law cannot be seen to make exceptions. And the crime is viewed all the more seriously because Andrew Beerton broke the time-honoured bond of trust that is supposed to exist between a servant and his employer. Anyway, on a much lighter note, I am pleased to say that Mrs. Van Allen is very much in your debt for what you did in helping to expose the robbery plan. She has invited you to call on her at your convenience, for she would very much welcome your advice on matters of style and taste. And she has lots of very wealthy friends to whom she is also prepared to introduce you."

Miss Freemont was clearly overcome to hear this. "Thank you, Mr. Holmes. That is indeed good news!"

"Yes," he replied, "but I think you have some good news of your own? If I am not mistaken, that is an engagement ring on your finger."

She blushed as he said this and went on to say that she had accepted a proposal of marriage from Gaston Lucien, the 28-year-old son of Charles Worth, her former employer. They were to be married the following summer.

I was stunned to hear the news, made all the more surprising because I had failed to notice the ring myself. I added my congratulations to those of Holmes and wished her all the very best for the future. When she came to leave, I walked her out of the house and once more insisted on hailing her a cab. It was with more than a touch of sadness that I waved her off, little realising it would be the last time I set eyes on that fashionably dressed young girl from Upper Brook Street.

3. The Whitechapel Butcher

One chilly evening in the March of 1883, Holmes and I returned from the theatre to find the upstairs study of our Baker Street apartment occupied by a burly fellow of the roughest hue. I was about to challenge the rogue when my colleague stepped forward and placed his hand ahead of me to halt my advance.

"My dear, Watson – let me introduce you to Mr. Henworth Paterson, diligent tradesman, purveyor of fine meats and a genuine *knight of the cleaver*."

Our visitor rose quickly from his chair, removed his ill-fitting cloth cap, and extended a huge hand towards Holmes. "Thank you, Sir. I hope you don't mind me waiting like this, but my business is somewhat urgent."

The tone of his voice was low and refined, belying his coarse appearance. He stood close to seven feet in height, his enormous upper body covered in a faded blue tunic over the top of which was tied a brown leather duck apron. His muscular lower limbs were clad in grey worsted leggings and on his feet were the largest pair of ankle boots I had ever seen. A mop of unkempt brown hair and whiskery sideburns framed the chiselled features of his long face.

"Not at all," replied Holmes, gesturing towards the chair.

Our guest resumed his seat and looked up quizzically. "How did you know who I was?"

"When I note that Mrs. Hudson has allowed an evening caller to enter her home and ascend the stairs, and has then offered him a cup of tea while he awaits the return of her lodgers, I anticipate that this is no ordinary visitor." He nodded towards the empty teacup on the small side table. "That you wear the livery so beloved of the *Whitechapel butcher* tells me your obvious profession. And knowing that Mrs. Hudson has purchased her meat from the same supplier for over ten years and refuses to shop anywhere else, it is but a small matter to conclude that you are the Henworth Paterson she speaks so highly of."

I fancied that I saw Mr. Paterson blush on hearing this and he smiled momentarily – a smile that was quickly replaced by a look of some concern. "Gentlemen, I will come straight to the point, for I am at my wit's end. I know something of your work from talking to Mrs. Hudson and thought that if anyone could help, it would be you. So I called this evening, explaining that I was desperate to seek your advice. And yet I could not tell that dear lady the nature of my anxiety - for I fear that tonight I shall murder a man!"

Holmes responded with no more surprise than if Paterson had announced that he had mislaid a favourite watch. "On that basis, I will ask Dr. Watson to pour each of us a large glass of whisky and must ask you to set before me the full details of how you have arrived at this most remarkable conclusion."

I busied myself doing as Holmes had requested and also offered Paterson a cigarette from a box on the mantelpiece. He readily accepted the scotch but declined to smoke. I lit one myself and settled back into the sofa. Holmes sat in an armchair facing the man and brought his fingertips together under his chin. Paterson took this as his cue to begin.

"I am now thirty-four years of age and have been a master butcher for some twelve of those years. I learnt the trade from my father, who passed away two years ago, leaving me the business. The shop has continued to provide me with a reasonable living, but I supplement the income with the rent I receive from two lodgers who live in the small rooms above the butchery. My wife, Louise, and I have our own living quarters downstairs at the back of the shop. I am devoted to her, and we share everything. When we married she put all of her savings into the business to allow us to take on other staff.

"We took in the first of our lodgers just after my father passed away. His name is Henry Rawlings, a middle-aged bookkeeper for the Great Eastern Railway; a quiet and meticulous man, who pays his rent promptly each week and sits down with us most evenings to enjoy a meal. Louise also takes in his laundry, and it has been Henry's custom since he arrived to pay a little bit extra for this and the meals he receives.

"Our second lodger, Ronald Moody, has been with us for just three months. He is five or six years younger than I and something of a gadabout. He works at a theatre in the West End and fancies himself as something of a stage performer. As well as a job in the booking office, he takes to the stage once or twice each week as 'The Great Ronaldo' entertaining audiences with his magic tricks and mind-reading shows. Unlike Henry, he has proved to be unreliable in paying his rent, and were it not for my wife's intervention on two or three occasions, I would gladly have shown him the door."

Holmes interjected at this point. "I know of 'The Great Ronaldo.' In fact, Watson and I attended one of his shows three or four weeks back."

I remembered the evening well. It had not been the most edifying of experiences.

Paterson continued. "About a month ago, I felt an enormous change come over me. I began to find it hard to get to sleep and to wake in the mornings and have felt continuously lethargic and anxious. Louise is convinced that I'm working too hard, as I routinely open the shop at five-thirty each morning and rarely close before seven in the evening. But other aspects of my behaviour have been more troubling. For it seems I have been sleepwalking into Henry Rawlings's room and trying to attack him."

"And you're convinced that this has something to do with the general change in your demeanour?" I asked.

"Yes," replied Paterson. "Prior to this, I have never experienced any ill-health and have always been able to sleep soundly."

Holmes seemed tetchy at the interruption. "Mr. Paterson, I would be grateful if you could explain specifically what has occurred, omitting no detail, however small it may seem."

Paterson nodded. "Each evening we sit down to eat at seven-thirty. Henry joins us for the meal most nights, while Ronald departs for the theatre. After the meal, Henry stays talking to Louise and reading his newspaper while I generally complete some of the paperwork and orders for the following day. My wife turns in at nine o'clock, by which time Henry has also headed upstairs to bed. But it has long been a habit of mine to leave the house at that time and to walk for a couple of hours before returning home. It helps me to clear my head and relax after a long day. I then take a large glass of strong Madeira wine before undressing, washing and getting into bed.

"On Monday the fifth of March, having followed exactly that routine, I woke in the early hours to find myself in Rawlings's room with a large steak knife in my hand. I was standing beside his bed as he cowered under the covers. Ronald had apparently come to Henry's aid and was trying to

52

persuade me to hand over the knife. I can't begin to tell you how embarrassed and concerned I was. I was relieved of the knife and began to apologise to Henry, admitting that I had not been feeling well. But to make matters worse, he then showed me a note which he said had been pushed under his door the previous evening. It read, 'I will kill you'."

Holmes sat forward in his chair and pointed towards Paterson. "Ah ha! A note which he believed *you* had written?"

Paterson nodded slowly. "There was no denying it. It looked to be in my hand and had been written on a sheet of headed paper torn from one of the butchery's order books – a book which I keep locked in a bureau at the back of the shop."

I had begun to scrutinise Paterson a little more closely with this revelation. The symptoms he had described and the reference to the death threat seemed to me to be strongly suggestive of his deteriorating mental state. Coupled with the obvious paranoia he was now demonstrating, I was inclined to believe that he might be suffering from the debilitating effects of mania, brought on by the long hours of work and his increasingly erratic sleep patterns. I had seen many such cases in both military and civilian life.

"That is most suggestive," said Holmes, reaching for his churchwarden and matches, "but how had Rawlings reacted to this earlier message?"

"He admitted that he had been most confused by it and had shown it to my wife. Louise had apparently reassured him that I had been feeling unwell and had been making mistakes and acting in ways that were out of character for me. On that basis, he had thought no more of it until he awoke that night to find me coming towards him with the knife. He had cried out in order to get Ronald's help. After I had been escorted back to bed, Louise and Ronald had convinced

Henry that this was likely to be an isolated incident which would not occur again."

"I see. And have there been other incidents since that time?"

"Sadly, yes. A few days later I took the decision to close the shop and let my three cutters go home early. It was probably around five o'clock that afternoon. Having locked the doors, I made my way through to our living quarters and was surprised to find Louise sitting beside Ronald and whispering something which I could not catch. Both looked up in surprise, and I saw Louise flush. Fearing that I had walked in on some infidelity on my wife's part, I was about to grab Ronald when he said that things were not as they looked. He then held up and passed to me a folded note which he said had been posted beneath Henry's door the previous evening. It read the same as the earlier message."

"And you were convinced once more that you had written it?"

"Yes, Mr. Holmes. I could think of no alternative explanation. And later when Louise and I sat alone to discuss the matter, she herself had to admit that the notes looked to be in my hand. She said that she had not wished to talk to Ronald behind my back, but was growing increasingly concerned about my health."

Hearing this, I was now even more convinced about my diagnosis and wondered if Holmes might be reaching the same conclusion. But he allowed Paterson to carry on and outline what had then occurred. In short, only two days after the appearance of the second note, Paterson had once more come around to find himself in Rawlings's room in the early hours, this time armed with a heavy cleaver. Moody had remonstrated with him to drop the weapon and order had then been restored. Unfortunately, Rawlings had not been inclined to let the matter rest and had approached the police that night, explaining what had occurred and presenting them with one of the notes that had been pushed under his door. The police had viewed the matter seriously, but had not taken any further action because Rawlings had announced later that he did not wish to press charges. Holmes seized upon this disclosure with some relish.

"What did you make of that, Mr. Paterson?"

"I was very relieved and grateful for the intervention of Ronald, who had accompanied Henry to the police station. He told me later that he had persuaded Henry to drop the charges, arguing that this was a medical concern rather than a criminal matter. Henry was unhappy with the situation and made it clear that he would go to the police again if any further incidents should occur. That was two days ago. For my part, I agreed to seek medical help and have arranged an appointment with a doctor for tomorrow afternoon."

"And yet you fear that the consultation may come too late. I take it that another of these mysterious notes has appeared?"

Paterson looked surprised. "Yes, but how did you know?"

My colleague responded somewhat wearily. "Something has clearly precipitated your fear that you are to commit murder this very night. It seemed most likely that this would be a third note."

Paterson fidgeted uncomfortably and then reached into the front of his apron, from which he withdrew a small, somewhat crumpled, piece of paper which he passed across to Holmes. My colleague regarded it keenly. Looking across from the sofa, I could see a message scrawled in large black letters on the headed paper. It read simply, 'I will kill you tonight'.

"When did Mr. Rawlings give you this?" Holmes asked, placing his churchwarden down in the hearth.

Paterson looked confused. "He didn't. It was an odd thing. Some time back, Ronald had mentioned to me that the ceiling above his bed appeared to be getting damper and he wondered whether there might be a leak in the roof. I agreed to investigate, but with all of the events I have described, had quite forgotten about it until this afternoon. Business was slow in the shop and when the matter came to mind I decided to leave one of my assistants in charge and to venture into the loft to see if I could see the source of the dampness. The entrance to the loft is in Henry's room. Had he not been at work, I would have been reluctant to approach it. But with a small ladder to hand, decided that this would be the best time to act, particularly as Ronald and my wife were also absent at that time. Having gone up into the roof space, I could see no discernible leak, so climbed back down through the hatch. As I was about to leave the room, I swung the ladder and knocked over a wicker basket beside Henry's desk. The contents were scattered across the floor so I had to tidy up the mess. I found *that* screwed up amongst the other bits of discarded paper."

Holmes beamed at our guest. "Indeed. And you can confirm that this headed sheet has also been torn from your order book?"

Paterson answered in the affirmative. Holmes then asked: "What do you make of it?"

Our visitor looked dejected. "I do not know what to make of it, Sir. I am consumed with fear. I cannot recollect writing such a terrible thing and yet cannot deny that it looks to be in my hand and set out on my own stationery."

I then asked: "What did the others say when you told them about finding the note?"

He shook his head. "I'll be honest, Doctor, I didn't raise the matter. I took the note and went back to work. Louise returned late in the afternoon and began to prepare the evening meal. Henry and Ronald both arrived back at about six o'clock. Nothing was said by any of them and, at Louise's invitation, both men agreed to join us later for the meal. Despite the circumstances, Henry seemed relaxed in my company and we talked amiably enough. But I could not help but think this was some play-acting on his part, with him knowing full well of the third note, yet choosing not to raise the matter with me."

Holmes rose from his seat and took a few steps over to the table near the window. He picked up a sheet of paper and an ink pen and handed them to Paterson. "Could you write, 'I will kill you' on this sheet?"

It took him but a few seconds to comply. When the sheet was passed back, the detective began to compare both messages, poring over each character with a magnifying glass. At the end of this examination he uttered just two words – "Most enlightening."

I sensed then that Paterson was beginning to get a little impatient. Holmes had clearly noticed this too, for he announced suddenly he had just two final questions. Firstly, he asked if our client had told anyone back at the house of his planned visit to Baker Street. When Paterson confirmed that he had not, Holmes then asked a most extraordinary final question: "While at your house, has Mr. Moody ever asked you to take part in one of his stage acts?"

Paterson seemed puzzled by the inquiry. "I'm not sure I understand what you mean, Mr. Holmes. Are you asking whether he has ever invited me to the theatre to assist him?"

Holmes clarified his line of enquiry. "No. I realise that I should not have talked so obliquely. What I need to know specifically, is whether Moody has ever offered to hypnotise you while at your house?"

Paterson looked at him incredulously. "It is odd that you should ask such a question, for I did at one stage wonder if my sleepwalking could be explained by that. Like you, I am well aware that Ronald occasionally uses elements of hypnosis in his stage act. When he first came to lodge with us, he told me as much, explaining that he is occasionally called upon to assist people outside of the theatre, for hypnosis can be used to treat certain conditions."

I could not help but interject. "Yes, it was the Scottish surgeon James Braid who first coined the term *hypnotism* in the 1840s. Like many others, he had discovered that a mesmeric trance could be induced in some patients by the use of a protracted ocular fixation. He believed that this left certain parts of the brain fatigued and in a state of 'neuro-hypnosis' and suggested that in this condition some individuals can be susceptible to influence and might be persuaded to alter their normal patterns of behaviour. This could be useful in the treatment of addictive or destructive behaviours."

Holmes seemed bemused by my interruption and asked the question again. "Did Mr. Moody offer to hypnotise you?"

Our visitor responded most definitively. "He did ask, explaining that hypnosis might help me to cope better with the demands of my work, without the need to rely on long evening walks and strong Madeira wine. But I told him I would never agree to such a request, however beneficial it might prove to be. I have no time for such quack remedies. I hope that does not offend you, Doctor?"

I laughed. "No, I take no offence. In fact, I share your concern. I believe it to be a pseudo-science at best, which could be misused by the unscrupulous."

"Then we are all agreed," concurred Holmes. "But in this case, it would appear that hypnosis was not the cause of Mr. Paterson's erratic behaviour. It seems we have some further work to do. I suggest that the three of us take a carriage to Whitechapel to continue our investigations. I believe it will be to our advantage that no one knows of our impending arrival."

As Paterson and I made our way through the door of the study and out on to the landing, I glanced back and saw that Holmes had paused to retrieve a magazine from his extensive archives. Smiling at me with a sly wink, he slipped the thin pamphlet in an inside pocket of his jacket and began to make his way towards the door. I had little doubt that the magazine would reappear later as our adventure unfolded.

****

It took us some time to travel across to Paterson's shop in Whitechapel. Even at that late hour the streets were awash with life and I noticed that a few shops and street vendors were still doing a brisk trade. As we bumped along in the four-wheeler, Paterson explained that many of his more unscrupulous competitors used the hours of darkness to sell off any meat which had gone past its prime. The aromas which had begun to fill my nostrils provided strong confirmation of this.

Holmes had spent much of the journey leafing through his magazine. When he eventually returned the document to his pocket, Paterson asked him directly: "Do you believe that I wrote those notes, Mr. Holmes?"

My colleague shook his head. "Not a bit of it. When I compared the note you had written for me to the writing on the sheet retrieved from Rawlings's basket, it was clear that the two did not match. The forgery was well-executed, but I am convinced that another hand has been at work. Beyond that, I cannot say more until I have further data."

Paterson seemed greatly relieved to hear this and turned back to me. I knew not what to make of the revelation, still believing that the butcher's mental state had some bearing on the case. A few minutes later we pulled up outside a baker's shop a short distance from the Paterson butchery and then continued on foot. Paterson led the way holding a small lantern he had brought with him to Baker Street. By means of a narrow side passage, we were able to approach the back of the shop quietly and discreetly. As Paterson unlocked the thick oak door to enable us to gain entry, I could see only one dim light in the middle of the three upstairs windows.

We followed our client into the property where he lit a couple of candles and then coaxed a gas lamp on a wall bracket into operation. I could see then that we were in a spacious kitchen and storage area containing two large sinks, a free-standing chopping block, some cupboards and shelves, and a large oak refectory table. Ahead of us ran a long passageway which I envisaged led to the butchery at the front of the property. On the left, some way along this, was a small staircase bathed in an orange glow. Paterson pointed to this and whispered that it led to a landing and the bedrooms of Rawlings and Moody. He then gestured towards a second stairwell in the corner to our right which provided alternative access to all of the upper rooms. A door beside this led to Paterson's living quarters.

There was not a sound in the property beyond the gentle ticking of a wall-mounted clock in the passageway. In a hushed tone, Holmes asked if he could first see the butchery's order book. Paterson tip-toed off down the passageway and returned a couple of minutes later clutching a blue and red bound book. Holmes placed it down on the chopping block and began to leaf through the stubs of the sheets that had been torn from the book. He then looked up and asked Paterson how the bureau was secured. Our client explained that the bureau was housed in a small office at the back of the shop and there were only two keys to its lock. One was kept in a secure cash till, while the other was attached to a key chain on Paterson's tunic.

Holmes then asked if Rawlings or Moody ever had reason to go into the shop. "No," he replied. "It is a condition of their tenancy that the shop space is off limits to them. Both men come and go using the stairs in the passageway and enter and leave the building using the door behind us. We take our meals in this main room and the lodgers have a small shared washroom just off the landing. They have no need to venture into the shop at all."

Seemingly satisfied with this new piece of information, Holmes then outlined his plan. Paterson was to rouse his wife from her slumbers and request that she go upstairs to bring both Rawlings and Moody down into the kitchen. If required, he was to explain that he wanted to apologise to both men for his recent behaviour. I was to stay hidden behind one of the larger cupboards until both men appeared and would then ensure that no one left the room. With no further elaboration, Holmes slipped away towards the second staircase in the corner of the kitchen and disappeared from view.

It took a good five minutes before Louise Paterson came through into the kitchen. Tucked into my hiding place I could hear her remonstrating with her husband about the unexpected interruption to her sleep. She seemed markedly reluctant to comply with his request to wake the lodgers, but eventually headed upstairs. Hearing her light footfall on the wooden stairs, I stepped out into the kitchen and took up a new position just out of sight of the passageway. Paterson took a seat at the table and waited for the drama to unfold.

The first to come down the stairs and into the kitchen was Henry Rawlings, who entered wearing a red dressing gown and black carpet slippers. Ronald Moody followed, dressed only in a thick cotton nightshirt, while Mrs. Paterson was clothed in a full-length night gown and wrap-around shawl. She too was wearing slippers and her long brunette hair was tied back with a blue ribbon. All three looked towards the butcher and while the men continued to stand, Mrs. Paterson took a seat at the refectory table. I then slipped out from my hiding place and stood before them saying nothing.

Rawlings seemed the most surprised. He was fair-haired, of slender build and approaching six feet in height. A thick moustache ran along his thin lip line and I could see that he had some considerable bruising around his left eye. He held my gaze. "Who is this, Henworth?" he asked quickly. The tone was accusatory. Paterson did not reply.

Moody then stepped forward, looking nervously between the two of us, before settling on the butcher. "Yes, who is this man?" He was also of slender build, clean shaven and boyishly youthful in his appearance. He looked very different to the man I had seen some weeks before on the stage. On that occasion he had worn thick theatrical make up.

Mrs. Paterson then intervened. "Henworth, please! What is the meaning of this? Have you finally lost your mind?"

62

To this point, none of the three had heard or observed the tall figure of Holmes, who now entered the kitchen behind them and stood commandingly by the doorframe, a piece of paper visible in his hand. "Perhaps I can answer some of your questions," he announced, startling Mrs. Paterson and Moody. "We have been called here to investigate the alleged threats to you, Mr. Rawlings. 'I will kill you' says this note; it was lying on the desk in your room. Is it evidence of Mr. Paterson's deteriorating mental state?"

"Are you the police?" asked Rawlings.

"I am a private detective, Sir." He waved his free hand towards me. "And this is my colleague, Dr. Watson. Now, what am I to make of this message?" He waved the note once more and then placed it in the left pocket of his jacket.

Rawlings's jaw was set hard as he answered. "I know not what trickery you are attempting to perform here this evening, but I will tell you that it is not the first time Henworth has threatened me with violence. On two previous occasions he has entered my bedroom during the night intent on assaulting me. And earlier this evening he once more accosted me in my room armed with a meat cleaver. The bruising on my face provides clear evidence of the attack. Had it not been for the timely intervention of Mr. Moody here, I would not have escaped with my life."

"Ah, then you witnessed this episode, Mr. Moody?"

The younger man looked at Holmes somewhat timidly. "Yes, I did. I heard the commotion in Henry's room and when I reached the landing could see Henworth brandishing the cleaver. Twice I saw him lunge at Henry. If you have taken that note from the room, you cannot have failed to notice the damage that has been done to the dressing table."

"Indeed, there is a most remarkable gash in the furniture. And I have no doubt that it was made by a meat cleaver. But what time did this incident occur?"

"It was close to eight-thirty this evening."

Henworth Paterson rounded on Moody and was about to rise from his chair, his fists clenched and his face crimson. Holmes intervened swiftly and placed a firm hand on the butcher's shoulder. "Please stay seated, Mr. Paterson. I believe we are getting to the nub of this matter, so would ask you to remain silent for the moment." Despite the man's anger it was clear that he trusted Holmes's judgement, for he resumed his seat and remained silent.

Holmes now turned to Louise Paterson. "Were you aware of this attempted assault, Mrs Paterson?"

She flushed and spoke quietly, "I did hear some commotion upstairs just before Henworth left the house for his evening walk. I was in my bedroom at the time, so did not get a chance to speak to him about it. To be fair, Henworth has not been himself recently, so anything is possible."

Her husband's head dropped at this point and he looked meekly towards the tiled floor of the kitchen. I still retained some doubts about his mental state.

"And nothing was said by your two lodgers?"

It was Moody who answered as the tears began to well in Mrs. Paterson's eyes. "We didn't feel it was the right time to tell Louise. But Henry has now determined that he must refer the matter to the police. The situation has got out of hand. Something has to be done."

Holmes regarded him for a few moments and then replied. "And yet you have not gone to the authorities. Why is that?"

Rawlings seemed agitated by the query. "We were waiting for Henworth to return home. We then planned to tell Louise about the assault and go to the police."

Holmes began to shake his head slowly from side to side. "This will not do! You tell me that you are planning to report an assault and yet the two of you were tucked up in your beds. This is all lies. So let me set the record straight. When Mr. Paterson left the house this evening he came to seek my assistance. He was concerned to know whether he had been sleepwalking and writing the threatening notes."

The bookkeeper stood his ground. "Good. And I'm telling you that his threats and attacks have been real enough."

Holmes took a couple of steps towards Rawlings and stared deep into his eyes. "You are lying, Sir, as I will prove shortly. Now, I want you and Mr. Moody to take a seat at the table beside Mrs. Paterson."

There was no resistance from either man and no further words exchanged as both moved to take their seats. Holmes then addressed our client. "Mr. Paterson. You mentioned earlier that you like to take a large glass of Madeira before retiring to bed each evening. I would be grateful if you could retrieve the bottle from your living quarters and bring it to me."

Paterson looked up in surprise. For a brief moment he seemed bewildered by the request but then nodded and rose from his chair. A couple of minutes later he was once again seated at the table and Holmes held within his hand a large bottle of the fortified wine. To the bemusement of us all, he removed the cork and began to sniff at the contents. He then took a small sip and appeared to be savouring the taste, before resealing the bottle and placing it on the chopping block beside the order book he had scrutinised earlier. From the passageway came the melodic chiming of the clock announcing the arrival of midnight. Holmes then began to speak.

"Mr. Paterson is a master butcher with an enviable reputation. He works hard and, like his father before him, does his utmost to serve his ever-loyal customers. And yet his diligence is not enough, for he is forced to take in lodgers to provide the additional income he and his wife require to live a decent life in this busy metropolis. Now, what if one of these lodgers had designs on the business and the income it affords? How might he go about removing our industrious butcher?"

Henry Rawlings pushed back in his chair and rose from the table. I braced myself fearing that he might launch himself at Holmes, but he just stood, red-faced and angry. "How dare you! What right have you to come in here and start flinging these wild accusations about in our home?"

Moody clearly felt that he too should offer up some challenge. "That is absurd, Mr. Holmes. If anything happened to Henworth it would be Louise who would take over the business. On what basis would Henry or I have any interest in the affair?"

Holmes raised his eyebrows and pointed at Mrs. Paterson. "For exactly that reason. Your phraseology is unfortunate, yet revealing – after all, one of you has been *conducting an affair with Mrs. Paterson.*"

There was an explosion of activity in the room. Henworth Paterson flung himself across the table towards Moody, clawing viciously at the front of the lodger's nightshirt. Rawlings began to use both fists to pummel the outstretched body of the butcher, while Mrs. Paterson jumped up, screaming wildly and tearing at her hair with both hands.

Holmes took it upon himself to wade in and break up the skirmish between the three men. I went to Mrs. Paterson's aid, calming her down and preventing her from harming herself further.

It was a good five minutes before order was restored. Mrs. Paterson continued to sob gently at one end of the refectory table. Her husband was seated beside the chopping block, while the two lodgers were slumped, somewhat dishevelled, in their original seats. I had taken a chair beside Mrs. Paterson, which left only Holmes standing and facing the two lodgers.

"Yes, I'm afraid that your wife is very much in the thick of this plot, Mr. Paterson. I suspected as much when you revealed who had access to the bureau where the order book is kept. Neither lodger could have routinely used the key from the locked cash till. And it would have been no easy matter to steal your key chain without the help of your wife."

The butcher cast Holmes a sideways glance and murmured, "I always suspected that Ronald was a little too close to Louise. He'll have put her up to this."

"On the contrary, it is Mr. Rawlings who is sweet on your wife. That much is obvious from the concerned looks they have been exchanging since we first arrived."

Paterson was clearly dumbfounded by the declaration, but did not move. His wife continued to weep. Rawlings laughed derisively and then said, "Perhaps if you'd shown more interest in your wife and less in your precious business, she might not have fallen into my arms. I had no intention of taking her from you, but the closeness grew as we sat talking each evening, while you went back to your orders. And the long walks before bedtime gave us further time together..."

Holmes cut him off. "This *closeness* has been going on for some time, hasn't it? Certainly before Mr. Moody arrived."

"I'm not ashamed to admit it. And in that time Louise has grown to despise Henworth, with his penny-pinching ways."

I was as stunned as Paterson to hear this and then asked a question of my own. "Was it Mrs. Paterson's idea to convince her husband that he was slowly losing his mind?"

Rawlings sneered at me contemptuously. "I'm saying nothing more. If you drag the police into this I can provide plenty of evidence that Henworth has been threatening to kill me and finally attacked me this evening. There are the written death threats, the damage to the furniture upstairs and the bruises around my eye. Mr. Moody will confirm everything I say."

My colleague snorted. "Of course he will. I would expect nothing less from your *younger brother*." He reached inside his jacket and withdrew the magazine he had been reading earlier in the four-wheeler. Flicking through the pages, he added, "I like to keep back copies of *The Stage* and have a keen interest in theatrical performers. Watson and I attended a less than impressive show given by 'The Great Ronaldo' some weeks back. I remembered reading something about the man in the magazine prior to that. Before coming here this evening, I located the article and looked back over it. Very instructive it was too. While he may operate professionally under the name 'Ronald Moody', the man beside you was born 'Richard Rawlings.' When I look at you together, there is no mistaking the familial similarities."

It was Moody's turn to look shocked. "It's no use, Henry. This gentleman clearly has the better of us. How he has fathomed it is beyond me, but I suspect he knows the full story. Am I right, Mr. Holmes?"

"I have a working hypothesis which I shall share with you. You may wish to correct any errors or omissions I make."

"We're all ears," retorted Rawlings with heavy sarcasm.

"The romance between Mr. Rawlings and Mrs. Paterson develops to the point where both feel they cannot continue to live under the same roof as Henworth Paterson. But having no particular money of their own, conclude that they cannot afford to move out and set up home elsewhere. Mrs. Paterson, in particular, has too much to lose, having invested all of her savings in the business. They cannot countenance the idea of murder, so set about devising a more cunning plan in which the butcher is cast in the role of villain. In short, they aim to convince the authorities that Mr. Paterson is in a fragile mental state, threatening – and actively trying to kill – Mr. Rawlings. Their objective is to see him imprisoned or removed to a criminal lunatic asylum.

"Mr. Rawlings hits upon a novel idea. His younger brother is a stage performer who routinely uses hypnotherapy as part of his act. He persuades Mrs. Paterson to convince her husband that they have a need for a second lodger. Knowing that Richard Rawlings uses the stage name 'Ronald Moody,' they are convinced that Mr. Paterson will not realise the two lodgers are in fact brothers. And with 'The Great Ronaldo' on board with their scheme, they set out to persuade the busy butcher that a course of hypnotherapy will benefit his health.

"Of course their biggest setback is that fact that Mr. Paterson absolutely refuses to go along with the planned treatment, so an alternative strategy has to be devised. Knowing that he likes to partake of a large glass of Madeira each night, a strong sedative is added to Mr. Paterson's wine. It has a soporific and mesmerising effect on him, such that Mrs. Paterson and the two lodgers are able to rouse him from

69

his bed in the early hours, walk him upstairs and place him in Mr. Rawlings's room armed with a weapon of their choice. They then bring him around and act out the charade that he has entered the room intent on harming the unfortunate lodger. To add further credence to their claim, Mr. Rawlings then begins to produce the forged death threats on headed pages torn from the butchery's order book.

"With everyone playing their part, they begin to achieve some success. And with the second of the faked incursions into Mr. Rawlings's bedroom, the plan is moved on. In short, the police are informed about Mr. Paterson's alleged threats and shown one of the forged notes, with Mr. Rawlings artfully deciding *not* to press charges at that time. It was a clever move, alerting the authorities to the fact that *something* was going on in the household, and providing early evidence that Mr. Paterson was in the thick of it."

Rawlings cleared his throat, causing my colleague to pause. "This is fanciful speculation, Mr. Holmes. Do you have proof for any of this?"

Holmes turned and pointed towards the chopping block. "Indeed. The Madeira wine has a faintly bitter taste. I will need to test it, of course, but feel certain that it contains a small quantity of laudanum. The opium alkaloids of the drug – the morphine and codeine in particular – would help to create the hypnotic effect experienced by Mr. Paterson and leave him increasingly lethargic and anxious during daylight hours. And as a reddish-brown liquid, it is easily disguised in red wine."

The bookkeeper appeared to have no response to this, so Holmes continued. "I am something of an artist myself when it comes to disguise, and so recognise how illusion and deception can be achieved by altering one's appearance.

While it is well-done, the bruising around your eye is nothing more than stage make up, applied – I imagine – by your brother, the theatrical performer.

"But it is the order book which contains the most crucial evidence against you. I have already suggested that Mrs. Paterson must have been involved in giving you access to it. You yourself forged the notes. I am something of an expert on handwriting and will be more than willing to present to a jury a compelling case as to why I believe the note taken from your desk and the earlier death threats are forged – particularly now that I have a comparable note written in Mr. Paterson's own hand."

He withdrew from his inside pocket the note which Paterson had replicated at 221B and explained how he had obtained it. He then retrieved the note which Paterson had brought with him to Baker Street and held it up alongside the first. "You will see that the hand in each case is remarkably similar, but to the trained eye there are at least six points of distinction between the two, leading me to conclude that they have been written by two different people. This second note, which is written on one of the sheets taken from the order book, was removed from the wicker basket in your room earlier this afternoon. Of course, you would not have known that, as Mr. Paterson did not discuss the matter with you and you did not raise the issue during your evening meal. The wording differs slightly from the earlier missives as it reads 'I will kill you *tonight.*' It is a subtle, yet significant difference, because it proves that you made a mistake and sought to correct the error. Had you later presented the note to the police, it would have cast doubt on your assertion that Mr. Paterson had slipped it under your door the previous night, as you maintained he had done on each previous occasion. Realising your error, you screwed up the note and discarded it in the basket, most likely planning to empty the contents later. You then wrote out another note, this time with the correct wording."

Moody interrupted. "How do you know that?"

Holmes walked across to where Mr. Paterson sat and placed the two notes down on the chopping block. "A good question, yet one which is easily answered. You see the order sheets are numbered sequentially. The discarded note was numbered 2571. I have the note which followed it." He withdrew a third sheet from the left hand pocket of his jacket and held it up for all to see. "This is the note which I took from the desk in Mr. Rawlings's room only a short while ago. If you look closely at the small number printed along the top of the sheet you will see that it reads 2572."

Moody looked unconvinced and threw out a further challenge. "I still don't see the relevance. It could be suggested that Henworth wrote both notes, particularly as you have now confirmed that he was in Henry's room earlier this afternoon."

This time it was Rawlings who responded, with some agitation. "Be quiet, Richard! The whole point of the notes was to suggest that Henworth was on the verge of lunacy and writing in a confused and sleep-like state. A man in such a condition is hardly likely to start rationalising how his notes might be interpreted and correcting his wording. There's no point denying what we've done."

It was an unexpected capitulation, after which Holmes sought to conclude the synopsis. "So having set the scene, you expected to conclude your plan this evening?"

"Yes," admitted Rawlings. "Henworth was to be led to my room once he had succumbed to the sedative. We'd already used the meat cleaver to damage the furniture and I asked my brother to create the bruising on my face using his theatrical make up. The note was to provide further evidence of Henworth's intent. With the police notified and all three of us sticking to our stories, I felt certain that we couldn't fail. Until you arrived, that is."

"Then there is nothing more I need to say. This will now become a police matter."

Henworth Paterson rose from his chair and glanced across to his wife, who continued to gaze down at the table. "I feel completely betrayed, Louise, but cannot see you languish in a prison cell for what you have done. You can dress, pack your bags and leave this house tonight, alongside these two." He pointed a thick finger at the lodgers, who also refused to look up. "I will not go to the police if you do as I say, but be clear about this – I never wish to see you again."

There was no doubting the resolve of the man. Mrs. Paterson made no attempt to remonstrate with her husband. Without a word, she rose from the table and headed towards her living quarters. The two lodgers also slipped away quietly to gather their belongings. Holmes took a few steps across to the butcher and placed a comforting hand on his shoulder.

"Thank you, Mr. Holmes. And you too, Doctor. I would not have wished for any of this, but thank you for getting to the bottom of it. There is a small thread of comfort knowing that I am not going insane. Beyond that, I have little to cheer."

We continued to stay with him for the time it took Mrs. Paterson and the two lodgers to pack their bags. There were no further words at their departure as the three left unobtrusively by the back door and slipped away into the night. We followed shortly afterwards, making it back to Baker Street as the first pale streaks of the new day emerged through the dawn.

We were later to learn from Mrs. Hudson that the Whitechapel butcher had opened the shop early the next day and had continued to serve customers in his usual meticulous fashion. And as Holmes had steadfastly refused to take any fee for his involvement in the case, Mr. Paterson insisted on filling Mrs. Hudson's basket each week with only the very best steaks, chops and sausages, all free of charge. As Holmes had stated earlier, Mr. Paterson was a genuine *knight of the cleaver.*

4. The French Affair

It was on a few sporadic occasions that my colleague chose to share with me tantalising details of the many adventures he had experienced during those three years of his self-imposed exile from May 1891. He had never made any secret of the fact that he had missed my companionship throughout that time, but I can only recollect one occasion when he admitted, somewhat candidly, that my absence had prevented him from solving a particular conundrum quicker than he might otherwise. He referred to the case simply as *The French Affair*.

"Watson, I fear that I have often taken your medical training and surgical knowledge for granted when you have stood squarely by my side," he confessed, looking thoughtfully into the burning embers of the fire. He took a further puff on his churchman and sent a plume of aromatic vapour high into the air above his head. "And yet, I had good cause to rue your absence and the inaccessibility of your considerable know-how during my short spell in Montpellier."

I glanced up from my newspaper and looked across to him. A look of genuine concern was etched across his face. "It is kind of you to say that, Holmes. But what was the nature of this Gallic challenge? In the past, you have hinted only that you spent some time working in a laboratory in the city. I know nothing more of the case."

He peered at me, smiled broadly and then jumped up from his seat with unexpected vigour. "Then I shall enlighten you, my friend." He pointed the stem of the pipe towards me. "It was not one of my better cases, but it did reach a point of some conclusion. I reflect on it only to illustrate the importance of having appropriate expertise near at hand. I will take you through the pertinent facts. You can then judge for yourself how you might have steered me as the case unfolded. I worked on the matter for a whole week. Had you been there, I suspect the investigation would have been considerably foreshortened."

I was flattered by his assertion and eager to hear the details of this enigmatic case. I placed the newspaper down by my side and picked up my whisky glass in anticipation. He then began to sketch out the nature of the affair.

"You will remember that having spent some time in Tibet and Persia, I eventually made my way to southern France at my brother's direction. It was Mycroft's belief that a semi-rural retreat would provide me with sufficient cover and protection from the Parisian underworld and any Continental associates whom Moriarty's loyal lieutenants might choose to enlist. Mindful also of my need to be intellectually stimulated, he arranged for me to take on a role as a chemist working for some French industrialists located on the outskirts of Montpellier. My research was focused on coal-tar derivatives and their potential uses. The task was not without its merits and I spent two pleasant weeks working diligently in the laboratory by day and whiling away my evenings in the bars of the Rue du Faubourg Boutonnet and the Opéra Comédie.

"The quiet isolation did not last long. In the third week of my sojourn, I received a telegram from Mycroft, addressed to me under my assumed name of Didier Laurant. He asked that I make contact with the mayor of Montpellier, whom I knew to be a close friend of his – in fact, the very man who had organised my sanctuary in the city. In short, the mayor had a problem which had threatened to escalate into a political catastrophe. Two days before, a wealthy retired merchant had been found dead at his château, having apparently died of a heart attack. But the doctor who examined the body had refused to issue a death certificate, expressing some concerns about the nature of the death and indicating that he could not rule out foul play. The Commissaire de Police was called to investigate and had concluded that the man had been poisoned by one of the domestic staff. He had strong suspicions that that culprit was a Spanish gardener – recently employed in the household – and had taken the fellow into custody. But without any conclusive proof, the mayor had been reluctant to bring charges against the gardener, fearing a backlash from the sizeable proportion of the city's population of Spanish descent."

I could not help but smirk. "So the mayor was content to put his electoral concerns ahead of any judicial priorities."

"Indeed. And what he wanted from me was a definitive view on the nature of the death and whether there was any real evidence against the gardener, who continued to be held in a police cell. In order to expedite the task, he arranged for me to lodge at the château until the matter was resolved. And to my very great annoyance, he explained to the Commissaire that I was a specialist detective from Scotland Yard who was on a short sabbatical to learn all there was to be learnt about crime detection in France! I collected the few belongings I had from my garret apartment in the city and was taken by carriage up into the hills where the Château Loire was situated.

"The small château had been built as a folly, no more than thirty years before. In addition to its impressive architecture, the formal grounds of the property included a vineyard, an arboretum, an orangery, and a large English-style garden. In fact, no expense had been spared by its owner, the wealthy Phillippe Laroche. As a widower, the eighty-six year old had lived alone, and was said to be a man of solitary and consistent habits. He rarely entertained visitors, would venture into the city but once or twice a year, ate a pre-planned menu each week, and followed a daily routine that was as predictable as it was short – he rose at ten o'clock each morning and retired to bed every evening at nine o'clock, following a short walk around his estate."

"Did his domestic staff not live in with him?" I queried.

"No, his aged housekeeper, Mlle. Lalande, was housed in a small cottage on the estate and had worked for Laroche for the previous twenty years. She walked up to the château every day; prepared, cooked and served his meals, and then retired each evening at seven o'clock. It was a routine which her employer insisted upon.

"A young maidservant, Rosalie Giroud, tended to the cleaning and domestic duties under the direction of Mlle. Lalande. She had joined the household staff five years earlier, when Madelaine Laroche had passed away, and lived with her parents in a village some two miles from the château. She always worked for seven hours, starting at ten o'clock each morning.

"The only other member of staff was the gardener, Carlo Cela, who had been at the château for just three months. He also lived on the estate, housed in a small lodge, and appeared to work every waking hour. He had been taken on because of his particular expertise in tending to vines. Blight had apparently laid waste to portions of Laroche's vineyard and Cela had considerable experience in treating *grape phylloxera*. Mlle. Lalande and Rosalie Giroud both confirmed that Phillippe Laroche had become very attached to the Spaniard. He had apparently taken to stopping by the lodge each evening, on his walk around the estate, to share a glass of cognac with the man and to discuss the general health of the gardens and vineyard. For his part, Cela had seemed very content in his new role and also got on well with the maidservant and housekeeper."

"Did Laroche have any children or other relatives?" I asked, noting that a wry smile spread immediately across my colleague's face.

"A key line of enquiry, Watson! Now, as it turned out, Laroche had no offspring and no known relatives. In fact, it might interest you to know that he had, only one week prior to his death, taken a rare carriage ride into the city to visit his solicitor. While there, he had amended his will. The new provisions allowed Mlle. Lalande to continue to live on the estate, rent free, for the rest of her days. And a very handsome legacy had been earmarked for Rosalie Giroud. That aside, who do you think was to inherit the estate and the bulk of his accumulated wealth?"

I spluttered while taking another sip of my whisky – "Surely, not the gardener?!"

"Yes, indeed! So you can begin to see why the Commissaire de Police believed he had a rock solid case against Carlo Cela. When I was granted an interview with the prisoner, he claimed to have no knowledge of the will, but did admit that he and Laroche had become very close, with the older man talking about him being the son he had always wanted."

I could see all too clearly, but wanted to know more about the circumstances of the death: "How was the body found and why did the doctor believe it was not a straightforward myocardial infarction?"

Holmes looked to be relishing the re-telling – his eyes wide and his gestures expansive. "I arrived at the château around five-thirty that afternoon, to be greeted by the amiable Mlle.

Lalande and one of the police officers assigned to the case. He obliged me by taking me straight to the scene of the death, explaining, as we ascending the grand staircase of the château to the owner's bedroom, that it was the maid who had discovered the body. Every day, at ten-fifteen, she had been required to carry a tray up to the room on which would sit a bowl of hot chocolate and some freshly-baked croissants. Ordinarily she would knock twice to then be invited by Laroche to enter the room. That particular morning she had knocked and received no such response. Knocking a second and then a third time, she knew that something was amiss and had tentatively opened the door to see the contorted body of Laroche laid out on the bed, his eyes fixated and his hollow cheeks displaying a livid and ghastly discoloration, as if some horror had confronted him prior to death."

The description prompted me to interject once more. "The symptoms quite clearly suggest a heart attack, but the real question is what gave rise to it. Tell me more about this discoloration on the face. Was the flesh jaundiced or flushed red?"

My colleague's face lit up once more. "That is exactly what I missed at the time, Watson! Your professional training prompts you to look, quite naturally and logically, at the symptoms as they are presented. It was the very question I should have asked as we approached the bedroom, but failed to do so, because I am not a doctor. Of course, I could not have observed this at the time, for the body had already been removed to a mortuary in the centre of Montpellier. So we will address your query shortly. For the moment, let me tell you what I observed on entering Laroche's bedroom.

"In proportion, the room was almost thirty feet square and positioned on one corner of the château; its four large windows providing extensive views out over the English-style garden to the front and vineyard to the right. It was furnished in a Spartan fashion, containing relatively few pieces for its size. Alongside a large oak-framed bed, this consisted of two rosewood bedside cabinets, an armoire wardrobe and an ornate cheval mirror, standing on a plinth. The room was flooded with light and there was only one other notable feature – the unmade bed on which had lain the body of the dead man.

"It did not take me long to conduct a thorough search. My French colleague confirmed that in addition to the maid, only he and the Commissaire de Police had entered the room. The windows were securely fastened and there was no visible evidence to suggest that anyone else had been in the room, although the door had no lock, so I could not be certain of that. On the closest bedside cabinet were positioned a number of items: a tall candle in its holder; a box of matches; a glass; a bottle of cognac and a small tin containing a quantity of white pills."

"Aha!" I cried, optimistic that the last item might indeed be suggestive. "And what were these pills?"

"Their brand name was *Antifebrin* and I was told later by Laroche's doctor that his patient had been taking the pills for over a year. The prescription had been given for the onset of facial neuralgia, which the otherwise healthy man had begun to suffer with. He would occasionally experience nervous tics down the left-hand side of his face and a twitching in one or both of his eyes. The pills had apparently helped with the condition."

"Yes, that is likely to be the case," I ventured. "Cahn and Hepp began producing these pills about five years ago – the acetanilide treatment has both analgesic and antipyretic properties. If he had been taking them for a year or more, it suggests that he had experienced no side effects from the drug. I can understand now why the bottle of cognac and glass were close by. The pills are usually dissolved in warm water and then swallowed, but can also be taken with spirits."

"Capital! Exactly as Laroche's doctor had suggested. Now, let us turn to the question you posed earlier. *What was the discoloration on the dead man's face?* It was only when I was granted permission to visit the morgue that this feature became apparent to me. I had expected the countenance to be crimson or streaked with red, but the skin had taken on a distinct bluish-purple tinge, which was also apparent on the extremities of the body – on the toes and fingertips. I recognised the significance immediately."

"Cyanosis," I added. "A discoloration of the skin or mucous membranes which results from the surface of the skin experiencing low levels of oxygen saturation."

"Precisely! But, of itself, no more suggestive of poisoning than the contortion of the body or the fixated eyes. And it did not rule out the possibility of a heart attack."

"Agreed. And had I been there, I would next have looked at the results of the post-mortem for some clarification."

Holmes sat at that point and placed the churchman down on the table beside him. "Again, your instincts serve you well, Watson, for I too should have been quicker to request access to the morgue. I will share the *post mortem* results with you in due course. But indulge me a while longer, for I wish to explain why the police believed poisoning to be involved and why they were content to point the finger at Carlo Cela. A search of the gardener's lodge revealed that he had in his possession a large mortar and pestle. Ground within the bowl, the police discovered small traces of a substance which, when tested, was found to contain the chemical *amygdalin*. You will recognise why they felt that to be significant..."

I was happy to oblige him. "Yes, the compound breaks down into toxic hydrogen cyanide and other chemicals within the human body. Cyanide poisoning would account for both the cyanosis and the related myocardial infarction. As a gardener, Cela is likely to have had ready access to many seeds from which amygdalin could be extracted. The mortar and pestle would be needed to release the chemical, which would otherwise remain intact within any seed casing."

My colleague nodded in approval. "A quick search of the garden revealed an ornamental hedge planted with wild cherry – otherwise known as English laurel – which produces such seeds. The Commissaire de Police believed this to be convincing proof that the gardener could have prepared the prussic acid capable of killing Laroche and had slipped it into the cognac which he gave to his employer that fateful night. He was wrong, of course."

It was my turn to smile. "I can guess now why you have, to this point, chosen not to share with me the findings of the *post mortem*. Had this been a genuine case of *cherry laurel seed poisoning*, there would have been a telling smell of bitter almonds in the stomach fluid and vital organs. You are about to tell me that no such aroma was detected."

"You have neatly anticipated the outcome, Watson. The autopsy revealed no such odour, thus weakening the case against the gardener. In fact, the stomach fluid was tested for a number of major poisons alongside hydrogen cyanide. All of the results were negative."

"And what was the police reaction to that?"

"The Commissaire refused to acknowledge the results, saying that the poison would have passed through Laroche's body many hours before, reducing the amount of prussic acid that was likely to be detectable."

"So he effectively overruled the doctor who carried out the autopsy?"

"Yes," admitted Holmes, "he was not the sort of character you would wish to argue with. And the mayor held him in high regard."

I had to admit that I was now totally fascinated by the case. Numerous questions kept springing into my mind. "How did the gardener account for the traces of prussic acid found in the mortar?"

My colleague reached over to pour himself a whisky from the decanter and topped up my own glass. "He was very direct in saying that he had used the mortar and pestle to prepare all sorts of remedies for treating garden pests and plant diseases. Some days before, he had prepared the crushed laurel seeds as an experimental treatment for grape blight, encouraged by his employer. I believed it to be very telling that he had not sought to clean the mortar. Had he poisoned Laroche, it seemed likely that he would have been keen to wipe away any traces of the crushed seeds."

Another thought occurred to me. "Was there any reason to suspect foul play on the part of the two women?

He shook his head. "No. As a precaution, the police arranged for samples of the hot chocolate and croissants to be tested for the same range of poisons. Predictably, the results were negative. Both women claimed to have known nothing of their employer's will and it was patently obvious that each had a considerable affection for the late Phillippe Laroche."

"Then I imagine at that point, you must have been inclined to believe that a regular heart attack was the most likely cause of death?"

Holmes swirled the whisky around in his glass and looked into it with an intensity of concentration. "You are right again. You see, I already knew by then that Laroche had died, not during the night – as the police had believed – but first thing in the morning, prior to the arrival of the maid."

"Was this again suggested by the *post mortem*?" I asked, knowing how much better my Continental colleagues were becoming at estimating the time of death in such cases."

"Partly," came the reply, "although the position of the curtains in the bedroom told me all I really needed to know." I must have looked confused, for Holmes looked across briefly, noted my expression, and then carried on. "I mentioned earlier that the bedroom was bathed in light. Laroche was not in the habit of sleeping with the curtains open. The police had assumed that Rosalie Giroud had opened the drapes when she entered the room. In fact, they had not even asked her the question. When I quizzed her on the second day of my investigation, the maid explained that her employer rose each morning, just a short while before her arrival with the breakfast tray, to put on his dressing gown and open all of the curtains. He had clearly done the same that particular morning."

"That is very revealing," said I. "It must have ruled out the possibility that he had been poisoned by the gardener. Had that been the case, the cognac and prussic acid would have been immediately evident when the contents of the stomach were examined during the *post mortem*."

"Yes, although the stomach fluid was found to contain a quantity of brandy..."

"...Taken that morning to wash down the neuralgia pills! I exclaimed.

"You have it, my friend! Now, where would you have gone from there?"

I raised my chin and thought carefully for a moment. "At that point, I think I would have refocused my attention on the pills beside the bed. Having discounted them earlier, the neuralgia tablets would have been well worth a second look."

"Bravo!" bellowed my colleague. "That is precisely what I did do, rather belatedly, on the morning of my third day at the château. I reasoned that if Laroche had arisen and taken a glass of cognac first thing, he must surely have done so to take one of the tablets. When I re-examined the *Antifebrin*, I realised something that I should have ascertained on day one – specifically, that this was a new prescription. The small print on the packaging indicated that a full tin contained one hundred pills. A simple count revealed that only one had been removed – the one taken by Laroche on the morning of his death. I know that if you had been with me, your professional curiosity would have led you to check that immediately."

I had to acknowledge that he was not wrong. In my medical career, a vast proportion of the inexplicable and suspicious deaths I had been asked to investigate were easily explained by reference to the medicine cabinets of those who had lost their lives. It was fairly standard practice to check prescribed doses against the amounts taken, or not taken, by patients.

Holmes then continued: "Armed with this new information, I decided to undertake some analysis of my own, wondering if the tablets had been tampered with in some way. I figured that if Laroche had been taking the same prescription for over a year, there had to be something different about these particular pills. I was taken by trap to my laboratory in Montferrier-sur-Lez and got straight to work. You can well imagine my surprise as I began to investigate the composition of the *Antifebrin*. It transpired that the compound was a phenolic coal tar derivative very similar to those I had been researching since first arriving in Montpellier. I spent two days testing pill after pill, after which I arrived at a startling conclusion. While the bulk of the tin contained pills of a standard composition, two were tainted with traces of a toxic organic compound..."

"Aniline, I imagine." This time it was Holmes who looked confused as I interposed. "A chemical consisting of a phenyl group attached to an amino cluster, which has more than a faint whiff of rotten fish. Inhaled or ingested by the human body, it has the potential to produce a number of toxic effects...most notably, cyanosis."

My colleague did not look in the least bit perturbed to have had the wind knocked out of his sails. "Watson, you never cease to amaze me. You are right in every respect. How did you know?"

I had to come clean. "Last month, there was a critical feature in *The Lancet*, which cast doubt on the efficacy of manufacturing acetanilide drugs. One of the major problems cited was the presence of aniline and the hunt is now on for a new breed of supposedly less toxic pain-killers and fever-reducing drugs."

"Well, well!" he chortled. "I wish I had known that at the time. It took me some hours to read up on the symptoms of aniline poisoning and to realise that Laroche's demise was a statistical fluke. Ordinarily, the quantity of aniline present in any tablet would have been insufficient to produce anything more than light-headedness. He just happened to swallow the one in a thousand which, when mixed with brandy on an empty stomach, led to more serious complications."

"So, you had your definitive conclusion – how did the mayor and the French police react to the news?"

"Well enough. I first took the precaution of revisiting the mortuary. One of the pathologists there re-tested the stomach fluid from the deceased and confirmed that minute traces of aniline were indeed present in the sample. Armed with this, I made my report to the mayor and the Commissaire de Police, who readily accepted that the death was due to misadventure. Carlo Cela was subsequently released from his police cell and returned to the château. The last I heard of the matter came from a conversation with Mycroft some months later. He told me that Cela had inherited the estate, married Rosalie Giroud and retained Mlle. Lalande as their cook."

"Then a happy ending for all three," I added. "And you had no further difficulties with the Commissaire?"

Holmes smirked and swallowed the last of his whisky. "No difficulties, as such. But he was a bright man with an enquiring mind who knew he had been outwitted. He realised from the first that I was no Scotland Yard detective. I had intended to leave the mayor's office after the meeting and return to my laboratory north of the city. The Commissaire followed me out into the street, determined to have the last word. He grabbed my elbow and held it firmly, before moving in close and whispering in my ear: 'It would be wise for you to leave this city, Mr. Holmes. You are too recognisable and I cannot guarantee your safety.' I still do not know whether this was a threat or a genuine concern for my welfare, but realised that my time in the south of France had come to an end.

"That night I packed my bags and headed to my next destination, little realising that the long rail journey from the

Gare de Montpellier would bring me into contact with one of the most diabolical assassins the world has ever seen."

I raised my eyebrows in astonishment and held his gaze. "And who was that?"

He reached for the churchman once more, placed it in his mouth and glanced around for his matches, which still sat, where he had last left them, on the right arm of his chair. "That, Watson, is an entirely different tale which I am loath to share with you at the present time." And with that, he relit the pipe, withdrew from further conversation and stared fixedly at the mantelpiece above the fireplace. I knew better than to interrupt him in that temporary place of refuge.

5. The Influence Machine

The early part of 1895 had already proved to be one of the busiest periods that Holmes and I had experienced in taking on the many cases and conundrums that presented themselves from week to week. And it was in June of that year that we were thrown unexpectedly into a short but ultimately unique affair which now deserves public attention.

I had returned to Baker Street that particular afternoon to present Holmes with a gift. Knowing his fondness for rare manuscripts on obscure topics, I had managed to purchase, at no great expense, a first-edition of Francis Hauksbee's 1715 lecture notes on *A Course of Mechanical, Optical, Hydrostatical and Pneumatical Experiments*. My colleague was immediately enraptured by the tome, flicking eagerly through its delicate pages and taking in the exquisitely printed diagrams which accompanied the text. It was a good twenty minutes before he re-engaged me in conversation.

"A most curious feature, Watson!"

I looked up from *The Times* and cast him a glance. I could see by his intense concentration that something inside the leather covering of the front cover had caught his attention. Slipping his bony fingers under an exposed section of the binding, he had withdrawn a small folded letter which he then began to scrutinise.

"This is most unexpected. You might remember that Hauksbee was the son of a draper. He ran a business off Fleet Street specialising in air-pumps, hydrostatic devices and reflecting telescopes. But as a scientist he is known principally for inventing an early electrostatic generator which he demonstrated at meetings of the Royal Society."

I had to confess, that beyond the name, I had little knowledge of Hauksbee or his work. "So what did this electrostatic generator do?" I asked, placing the newspaper down on the arm of my chair.

"The contraption consisted of a sealed glass globe which could be rotated rapidly by a hand-cranked wheel. While spinning the wheel with one hand, Hauksbee would use his other hand to place a light cotton cloth on the top of the rotating glass. The electrical charge he created would produce a light which stunned everyone in his packed lecture theatres."

"Most fascinating. And was the note that you now hold in your hand written by Mr. Hauksbee?"

He smirked mischievously. "No, that is the curious feature!" He was in a state of some excitement and rose from his chair to retrieve a magnifying glass from the mantelpiece. He then sat at the table before the window and began to examine the document through the lens. "A short, personal note, written on cheap paper. The high concentration of cotton fibres suggests it was manufactured close to one of the Northern mill towns. The watermark is crude but reveals the words 'Lewden Mill.' My supposition is thus confirmed – the paper mill is in Worsbrough, Yorkshire."

I was, as ever, stunned by his ability to retrieve such trivia from the depths of his memory. "What else can you discern, Holmes?"

"This is a non-standard paper size and the residue of gum along the top is most suggestive. It has been torn from a notepad. Possibly one used by a professional man. It is written in cheap black ink, which has faded considerably over the years since this was written. The hand is free-flowing, but lazy – undoubtedly that of a person well-used to firing off short missives. It will not surprise you to learn that the author is a medical man."

I coughed unexpectedly at the disclosure. "Really! You gathered that from some black ink and the style of handwriting?"

My colleague grinned once more. "No, he's signed it 'Owen Douglas, MD.'"

We both laughed and Holmes went on to reveal more. "It's dated '12th March 1884' and starts simply, 'To my dearest James,'. The address of the intended recipient is 7 Crescent Grove, Clapham Common. As for the contents, you had better read those yourself."

I joined him at the table and was handed the note. It read:

Please accept this book (one that I remembered you had wanted for your collection) as a small token of my appreciation for what you have given me.

I used the Influence to re-start the heart of a local man, Wright Littlewood, who had suffered a heart attack. He has recovered admirably, but I will keep you informed of his progress.

I am loath to broadcast my success more widely, for fear that it may be deemed to have been a dubious professional act. However, I am now even more convinced that your invention has the power to save lives.

I am forever in your debt and remain,

Yours faithfully,

"Well, what are we to make of it, Watson? Is it not a most baffling, yet fascinating, memorandum?"

"It is," I replied, "I know that others have claimed success in using electricity to resuscitate patients. In 1774, a country doctor claimed to have applied an electric shock to the chest of a young girl to re-establish her pulse. Since then, many have carried out experiments on the power of defibrillation, albeit mainly on animals. Most recently, in the 1840s, the Italian physicist, Carlo Matteucci, published his studies into the electrical properties of animal tissue. So the idea that a doctor could successfully induce ventricular fibrillation using shock treatment is within the realms of possibility."

"Excellent!" exclaimed Holmes. "Then let us assume for the moment that the incident referred to is genuine. The note is a personal one, so we have the task of discovering who 'James' is or was."

"Well clearly he is also a medical man," I ventured.

"It would be tempting to think so, but the use of the word 'invention' makes me wonder if our man might be a pioneer in a broader field. That he wanted to own a copy of the Hauksbee book further suggests that his interests may be more scientific and mechanical rather than medical." He pointed once more at the note before us: "And there is something about the use of this term 'Influence' – I believe I am right in saying that some of the electrostatic generators that have been developed in recent years are sometimes referred to as *Influence Machines*."

"That may well be the case, but where does that leaves us? Without a surname, we may still be on a wild goose chase. In any case, Holmes, are you really intent on pursuing this given all of the other demands on your time?"

I could already tell what his answer would be. When my colleague was fired up to this extent he was hard to dissuade. "There is more to this matter than we have yet discovered. And you forget – we have an address!"

"But how do you know that this fellow has not died and his book collection has been sold or given to the dealer I purchased it from?"

"A good point, my friend. And one that is easily checked. Let us test your theory. What was the name of the book dealer?"

"It was Bumpus's on Oxford Street."

"Splendid, then we will take in some fine London air and enjoy a stroll on this particularly pleasant afternoon."

∗∗∗∗∗∗∗∗∗∗∗∗∗∗∗∗∗∗∗∗∗∗∗

It was less than a mile to the bookshop. The capital was bathed in warm summer sunshine and the temperature had soared. Walking at the pace dictated by Holmes, I found it uncomfortably clammy, clad as I was in a thick tweed jacket with matching waistcoat.

I took the opportunity to fire questions at Holmes in an attempt to slow him down, but the quest proved fruitless. "How do we know the book wasn't stolen?" said I, breathlessly.

"The Bumpus family members are reputable dealers – their business is built upon that. They will keep records or know where all their stock comes from," he shot back at me. "Now, come on, Watson, keep up!"

Once inside the large book shop, it took me just a few seconds to spot the assistant who had sold me the book earlier that day. He was most helpful, if not a little concerned at first that I wished to return the book. Having satisfied him on that score, Holmes explained the nature of our quest, saying that we had discovered a personal note within the cover of the book and now wished to return it to the book's original owner. *Could he therefore tell us anything about where the book had come from?*

The subterfuge worked perfectly: "The book was brought in the previous week by a well-dressed man of about sixty. He had only the one volume to sell. Naturally, before agreeing to buy the manuscript, I asked him why he wished to sell. In response, he said that he knew the book to be collectable and of great value to those with a mind for science. As such, he was loath to dispose of it. But for very personal reasons, he could no longer bear to hold on to it."

"I see," said Holmes. "And did the man give any indication of where he lived?"

"Yes. I think I remember him saying something about travelling in from Clapham Common."

"Excellent! Then we will not trouble you further. For that is indeed our man!"

The assistant seemed slightly disconcerted by Holmes's exuberance, but, when thanked, bade us, "Good day then, Gentlemen," as we headed for the door.

Out on the street, Holmes was elated. "Our man is still alive, Watson! It just remains for us to pay him a visit. Then, hopefully, all will become clearer."

"I wonder what these 'very personal reasons' were for wanting to sell the book after a decade or so."

"That we cannot know until we speak to him," replied Holmes. "Now, we will catch a cab back at Baker Street.

Before we make the journey out to leafy Clapham, there is something I must just check.

Holmes insisted on leaving me out on the street when we made it back to 221B. He had only been gone for some six or seven minutes when he re-emerged from the door, a broad grin lining his face.

Sat within the interior of a hansom cab a short while later, he explained: "I am getting sloppy with age, Watson. Had I checked my trade directories earlier, we would have discovered that our man was indeed still alive. A quick search of the address revealed that the occupant of 7 Crescent Grove, Clapham Common is none other than a James Wimshurst. Interestingly, I could find no doctor by the name of Owen Douglas registered in the county of Yorkshire. If necessary, I will check later whether there is a doctor of that name elsewhere in the country."

****

It was a six-mile cab journey out to Clapham. I was surprised by how much the area had changed since I had last ventured there. Alongside the grand mansions in Old Town and those that fronted the common, there were newer developments, including those of Crescent Grove and Grafton Square.

The cabbie set us down outside the large gates of 7 Crescent Grove. It was an impressive building set within a fair-sized plot. Holmes wasted no time in passing through the gates and heading up the gravel drive towards the grand doorway. At the door, he pulled on a bell cord and some moments afterwards we were greeted by a thin, wan-faced maid. Holmes presented his business card and we were told to step inside while the master of the house was informed of our arrival.

The James Wimshurst who came to greet us was an affable fellow of medium build, with a full, greying beard and balding head. He instructed the maid to arrange for some tea to be brought to his study and invited us to follow him to the room, which sat across the entrance hallway to the left.

Inside the study we could see that he had something of a passion for scientific and mechanical devices. On every surface stood telescopes, small steam engines and strange globes containing wheels, cogs and metal wiring. Framed around the walls were engineers' drawings and technical charts, and in the bay window was housed a large collection of reference books, all of a scientific or technical nature.

Wimshurst was the first to speak. "It is indeed a pleasure to meet you, Mr. Holmes. I enjoy reading of your exploits. And I am hoping that this is your chronicler, Dr. Watson?"

I nodded and having shaken hands, Wimshurst invited us to take seats around a small oval table. At Holmes's request, he then explained the nature of his work. He had been born in Poplar and was apprenticed as a shipwright. Following a move to Liverpool, his career progressed rapidly and he had eventually become the chief shipwright surveyor for the Board of Trade at Lloyds.

Encouraged to say something about the assortment of devices scattered around the room, Wimshurst beamed and explained that he devoted much of his free time to experimental works. He had invented a vacuum pump which enabled the stability of ships to be determined and had experimented with ways of electrically connecting lighthouses to the mainland. But in the late 1870s he had begun to focus on his real interest – the creation of electrical influence machines for generating electrical sparks for scientific purposes. He went on to say that he had a well-equipped workshop in the garden containing all of the tools and instruments he treasured.

With these pleasantries completed and the arrival of the tea tray, Holmes then took the lead, keen to explain the nature of our visit. He withdrew from a pocket the note written by Dr. Douglas, opened it and placed it on the oval table in front of Wimshurst. The demeanour of our host changed immediately. He looked visibly shaken, his hands began to tremble and tears began to well up in his eyes. As he looked up from the note towards Holmes, he could only whisper, "Where did you get this?"

Holmes apologised for his abruptness in revealing the document. He explained how he had been given the Hauksbee book as a gift and had discovered the note tucked within the leather binding of its cover. He then added, "I sincerely hope you will forgive us, Sir, but we wished only to discover the story behind the note. If you would prefer us to leave, we will of course do so."

Wimshurst had begun to regain some of his composure. He smiled weakly and then replied. "Gentlemen, this has come as something of a shock. I had no idea that the note was still with the book. It must be a good ten years since I received both from my good friend Owen Douglas. It was only last week that I sold the manuscript, for I could no longer bear to have it in the house."

I did my best to ease the tension. "Yes, Mr. Wimshurst, we called in a Bumpus's and were told that you had sold the book for personal reasons."

"That is something of an understatement. I will do my best to outline the story for you. You may then understand why I felt it necessary."

He took a final sip of his tea and placed the cup down on the tray. "After the move to Liverpool, my wife and I became acquainted with a young country surgeon named Owen Douglas. He had a thriving medical practice in the town of Lepton on the outskirts of Huddersfield. Owen was something of a medical pioneer and shared my interest in all things mechanical. Like me, he collected rare scientific texts.

"For the three years from 1880 I began to work on a new type of electrostatic generator, capable of producing very high voltages. The influence machine was very different from some of the early generators I had worked on which relied on friction to produce an electrical charge. My machine was constructed with two large insulated contra-rotating discs mounted in a vertical plane; two crossed neutralising bars with wire brushes; and a spark gap which was formed by two metal spheres. In this way, an electrical charge is separated through electrostatic induction, or *influence*, rather than friction.

"The new generator proved popular with many other scientists and engineers. Douglas was particularly enamoured with the device and insisted on taking possession of one of my early working models. He also tried to get me to take out a patent for the machine, but I resisted this fearing a legal challenge from others who were working in the same direction.

"Throughout 1883, Owen began to tinker with the machine believing that he could use it for some of his pioneering medical treatments. He was convinced that small electrical charges could be used, for example, to stimulate damaged nerve tissue. He would write to me on his progress, but insisted that I keep quiet about his work, fearing that he might be struck off by the British Medical Association for unethical conduct.

"In March 1884, he believed he had achieved some success while operating on a worker who had been injured in an accident at a local meat factory. Wright Charlesworth Littlewood was a 36-year-old tripe dresser who had been badly wounded with a cutting machine. He was carried from the factory to Owen's surgery in a terribly weakened state, having lost a significant quantity of blood. On the operating table he then suffered a heart attack and stopped breathing. Alone with his patient, Owen believed he had but one hope to save Littlewood. With his adapted electrostatic generator in full motion, he sent a sizeable electrical charge into the man's chest and was stunned to find that the heart had indeed restarted. The note you have before you, Mr. Holmes, was written that evening."

I was amazed to hear this and gripped by his narrative. I was both shocked and awed to hear of the surgeon's conduct, but recognised that I too had occasionally resorted to unorthodox practises in an effort to save men on the battlefield. I was therefore in no position to sit in judgement on the ethics or efficacy of the man's approach.

Holmes took the opportunity to ask a direct question. "I take it that this Wright Charlesworth Littlewood survived the ordeal?"

Wimshurst gave him a solemn look. "Sadly, yes."

It was not the response I had expected to hear, and our host had evidently noted my look of surprise. "You must forgive me, Dr. Watson, but there is much more to tell. Littlewood was patched up and confined to bed for many weeks. Slowly, with the support of his wife, Helen, the man recovered and eventually went back to work. In time, he opened up his own meat factory with some success.

"Owen was delighted to see Littlewood recover. He wrote to me frequently in the weeks and months that followed convinced that my influence machine had real potential for saving lives. But try as he might, he was never able to replicate the outcome he had achieved in the factory worker's case. With the passage of time he shifted his attention to other ground-breaking surgical work."

"And how did you feel about the incident?" I asked.

"At that time, I was thrilled to think that the influence machine had saved a life and might have a medical application. And every time I leafed through the Francis Hauksbee manuscript, I was reminded of Owen's work and the close friendship we shared. That was all to change in December 1892..."

"...when Wright Charlesworth Littlewood was found guilty of the murder his 16-year-old daughter, Emily."

It was Wimshurst's turn to look surprised. "Then you know of the case, Mr. Holmes?"

My colleague answered him directly without conceit. "I have made it my business to study the details of all major criminal cases in recent years. The man's name was so unusual that I felt it could not be a coincidence. As I recollect, the factory owner lived with his wife and daughter in the village of Honley. Emily was a sickly child of no great intellect and prone to epileptic fits. She was never allowed to leave the home on her own. Susceptible to bouts of depression and suffering from his addiction to alcohol, Littlewood slit her throat one night and was tried for the murder. He was found guilty by reason of insanity and is currently detained within the Broadmoor Criminal Lunatic Asylum in Berkshire."

The solemn look had returned to Wimshurst's face. "All true, I'm afraid. And the case was to have a devastating impact on poor Owen. It was talk of the villages around Huddersfield and one or two people remembered that the surgeon had once saved Littlewood's life. Sinking into depression he began to blame himself for what had occurred, believing that he had committed an unnatural act in using the influence machine to revive Littlewood's heart. Twelve months ago he took his own life, convinced that he had been wrong to try to play God all those years before."

I could not hide my dismay. "That is a truly distressing story. I can understand now why you took the decision to sell the Hauksbee book."

"Thank you, doctor. After Owen's death I could not bear to see the book in my library. I just hope that it gives you more pleasure, Mr. Holmes."

Holmes rose from the table and extended his hand towards Wimshurst. As the two men shook hands my colleague made a final, telling comment. "Sir, you must not let this dreadful business dent your faith in science and technology and its potential to change the world for the better. We need men and women like you; the inventors, the pioneers and the free-thinkers. Our progress as a species depends upon it."

For much of our journey back from Clapham, Holmes and I sat in silence, each mulling over private thoughts and reflecting on the heart-rending nature of what we had discovered. This had been a short interlude in a year which saw the two of us engaged in numerous assignments, travelling the length and breadth of the country in pursuit of the strange, the criminal and the inexplicable. But it was an episode which Holmes was never to forget. A few days after our trip to Clapham, a boxed package arrived at Baker Street, addressed to my colleague. Inside was a perfect working model of the 'Wimshurst Machine'. Alongside the Hauksbee manuscript, it was a gift he treasured for the rest of his life.

Note: Readers may like to know that between 1899 and 1900, Jean-Louis Prévost and Frederic Batelli – two physiologists from the University of Geneva – first demonstrated a device that used small electrical shocks to induce ventricular fibrillation in dogs. It was a forerunner of the modern defibrillator. I was fortunate enough to meet both men at a medical conference in 1902. I do not know if James Wimshurst knew of their endeavours. Sadly, he passed away in the January of 1903. – JHW.

6. The Spectral Pterosaur

Compared to many of his police colleagues, Inspector Stephen Maddocks was an infrequent visitor to Baker Street. Seldom would he admit to being stumped or outwitted on a case. When he needed help within Scotland Yard it was usually to his old school chum, Sergeant Vincent Fulton that he deferred. But on the very rare occasions he required external assistance it was always to Sherlock Holmes he turned. So it was that on a cold Friday evening in the October of 1889 the dutiful inspector called in at 221B to consult with my friend and was shown up to the first floor study.

"An unexpected pleasure, Maddocks – please take a seat. Would you like a cup of tea or something a tad stronger?"

The detective ambled slowly and uneasily towards one of the armchairs, removing his brown Derby and long black overcoat. I stepped forward to take both from him which elicited only a weary and somewhat absent-minded, "Thank you, Doctor." He sat heavily, and I noticed that he had gained some weight since we last met. "A large brandy would be much appreciated."

I declined the offer of a glass myself, while Holmes poured a small measure of his own and then sat in a chair close to the hearth. "Now, how can we assist you?"

The poor fellow looked dog-tired, his eyes bloodshot and the skin beneath them dark and puffy. There was a distinct wheeziness in his breathing and a slight rasp to his voice. His face was flushed with pink. Having downed the spirit in one, he placed the glass upon the side table to his right and responded: "Sergeant Fulton and I have been investigating the theft of some rare museum artefacts, mainly preserved animal bones. *Fossils*, I believed they're called. A number of private collections have also been raided, so we have been told to leave no stone unturned in catching those responsible. Apparently, these old bones are irreplaceable and worth a lot of money..."

He coughed deeply and brought his fist up to his mouth. An uncomfortable silence followed which I felt obliged to fill. "Yes, Inspector. Palaeontology is a relatively new science, but interest in it has grown since Charles Darwin first published his book, *On the Origin of Species*, in 1859. Since that time, men of science have been scouring the planet to unearth the preserved remains of prehistoric creatures to confirm or refute his theories about *evolutionary biology*."

Maddocks spluttered once more and interjected. "Well, that's as maybe, Doctor. All I know is it's a terrifying business I've experienced – an unearthly vision – and I find myself completely baffled. In all the years of my service, I cannot recall seeing anything remotely like it..."

Holmes waited for him to elaborate, scrutinising the face of the police officer with evident intent. But there were no further words. Maddocks sat rigidly in the armchair, his eyes wide, his gaze fixed and his mouth poised to continue. Whatever inexplicable narrative he had planned to relate was not forthcoming.

I was quick to spring into action, recognising before my colleague that all was not well. Maddocks had stopped breathing and I could detect no pulse in his left wrist. For the next few minutes I tried in vain to resuscitate him, but eventually conceded that nothing more could be done. Already I could see that the skin on his face had taken on a deep crimson hue. Added to the rigid contortion of his body, it was clear to me that he had suffered an immediate and fatal heart attack. Having undertaken his own brief examination, Holmes concurred.

We sat for some time in silence, both overwhelmed by the drama we had witnessed. While he could be detached and methodical in times of heightened tension, I could tell that Holmes was deeply troubled by Maddocks's departure. The unsettling emotion prompted him within minutes to focus instead on the cold comfort of the logical, and the facts at hand.

"I think we had both noted that the inspector was not in the best of health on arriving here this evening, but I would not have expected such a rapid deterioration and expiration. Perhaps this 'unearthly vision' he referred to has sent him to his death." He stared into his brandy glass. "Although, of course, we should not rule out poison at this stage."

I stared at him incredulously, "You cannot mean that the brandy is poisoned?"

Despite the solemnity of the occasion, Holmes smiled. "No, Watson. As you can see, I am perfectly fine, having drunk from the same bottle as the inspector. I suggest only that we must be sure of our facts and eliminate all of the possibilities with a few toxicology tests. Procedurally, of course, we must contact Scotland Yard and let them handle all of this. But we must impress upon the doctor called to undertake the *post mortem* that this may not be a straightforward death."

Holmes wasted no time in despatching a short telegram to Scotland Yard's 'B' Division explaining what had happened and requesting that a pathologist be asked to accompany any investigating officers. It was a good two hours later when the heavy footfall of boots could be heard ascending the seventeen stairs to the first floor. Holmes opened the door of the study and ushered in three tall gentlemen in heavy overcoats.

"Ah! Inspector Bradstreet and Sergeant West. Good evening, gentleman." He nodded towards the last of the trio. "And this must be our medical man."

The police surgeon had no time to answer before I stepped forward and interrupted, offering him my hand. "Doctor Lorrimer, it is a pleasure to meet you again. Doctor John Watson, formerly of the 5th Northumberland Fusiliers – you may remember that we worked together briefly some ten years ago before I made the passage to India."

His face lit up in recognition and he extended his hand towards me. "Indeed I do, sir. I spent a year at the Royal Victoria Hospital. And I remember that while you were with us at Netley for just a few months, you made a great impression." He looked towards Holmes. "Of course, your life has taken a distinctly different course since that time."

I was unsure what he meant by this but let the matter rest. When we were all seated, Holmes explained briefly what had occurred earlier in the evening, although I noted that he failed to mention the inspector's reference to the 'unearthly vision.' Dr. Lorimer took his leave and went across to examine the body which we had laid out on a table beside Holmes's chemical apparatus. I felt obliged to go with him, but continued to listen carefully to the conversation behind me.

"A glass of brandy, you say, Mr. Holmes?"

"Yes, Inspector. I poured Maddocks a large measure at his request."

"I see. Well I think we'd best take the bottle with us. Not that I'm setting hares coursing you'll understand. We just need to be thorough."

"Of course," replied Holmes. There was more than a hint of sarcasm in his tone.

Sergeant West had evidently risen from his chair to retrieve the bottle from the table near the window. "How can we be sure that no one has tampered with this, sir?"

It was my turn to pour scorn on the proceedings. I spun around to face the group. "I can assure you Sergeant that Holmes and I have acted with the utmost professionalism in reporting this matter and laying the facts before you. Are you suggesting that we had a reason to want Maddocks dead and have sought to cover something up?"

West looked sheepish but remained silent. Bradstreet then intervened to restore some accord. "No one is saying that, Doctor. But we must follow procedures. The death of a police officer while on duty is always considered a very serious matter."

Holmes interposed. "You say that Maddocks was still *on duty* when he visited here this evening? I had assumed that he had completed his shift, for I have never known him to accept any form of alcoholic beverage while working."

Bradstreet looked bemused. "Yes, he and Sergeant Fulton had been sent to the British Museum's Natural History building to ensure that its collection of fossils and dinosaur bones remained secure. After all the recent raids, the curator at the museum feared they might be targeted next."

"And is Fulton still at the museum?"

"As far as I know." He pulled his fob watch from his waistcoat and glanced at the time. "They were due to finish their shift at ten o'clock, so Sergeant Fulton still has well over an hour until he stands down."

"In that case, might I suggest we make our way to the museum and quiz Fulton about events earlier this evening?"

Bradstreet nodded. "Certainly. I had hoped to speak to Fulton when he returned to the station, for he will be unaware that Maddocks has passed away. The two have always been close. I think it best if I break the news first, before we all descend on him."

There was general agreement to this. Lorrimer, West and I then attended to the body, struggling to manoeuvre the corpse from the study and down the stairs. Inspector Bradstreet had clearly thought ahead, for a covered police wagon was sat outside the house, fronted by two large horses. Its driver jumped down on seeing us and helped to carry the body to the back of the vehicle. Lorrimer and West climbed into the back of the wagon to accompany the cadaver back to the police morgue, the doctor inviting me to attend the *post mortem* the following morning. When the wagon had departed, Bradstreet, Holmes and I set off to walk the three miles to Cromwell Road.

It was a chilly night and a thin layer of mist hung in the air. By the time we reached Hyde Park it was difficult to see for more than a few yards in any direction. For the most part we walked in silence, with Bradstreet making occasional remarks about the quickest route to the museum. I could sense Holmes's annoyance at this, for no one knew the streets and geography of the capital better than he.

We arrived at the museum a little before ten. Knocking at the main entrance we were greeted by a night watchman who explained that Sergeant Fulton had been on duty for some hours and could be found in the vaulted central hall. As agreed, we let Inspector Bradstreet go ahead of us to inform Fulton about his colleague's demise. Some minutes later the inspector returned and said that Fulton had taken the news as well as could be expected and was comfortable to talk to the three of us about events earlier that evening.

Holmes and I had met the muscular Vincent Fulton on only one previous occasion. Some months earlier, the Yorkshireman had accompanied Inspector Maddocks to Baker Street when the pair had been seeking information about Gabrielle Cavellaro, a volatile Italian anarchist, whose notoriety as a bomb maker had made him the toast of the London underworld. Shortly after getting involved in the case, Holmes had surprised me one day by announcing that Cavellaro no longer posed a threat. Pressing him for further information, my colleague had added only five words: "He had a short fuse."

The police officer that stood before us now looked to have none of the self-confidence that he had displayed on his visit to 221B. It was clear that Fulton had taken the news of the death badly. His face was ashen and his eyes betrayed the deep shock he had experienced. It was all he could do to nod and acknowledge our arrival as we joined him in the main hall and shook him by the hand.

We stood at the foot of the magnificent stone staircase surrounded by the most incredible exhibits I had ever set eyes upon. With more than a passing interest in recent discoveries, I could see the preserved remains of various species, including *Iguanodon*, *Hylaeosaurus* and *Megalosaurus*. In a long glass case to my right was the preserved skull of an Ichthyosaur. I remembered that the renowned anatomist, Sir Richard Owen, the first director of the British Museum, had first coined the term *Dinosaurus* from the Greek words for *terrible* and *lizard*. And in a lecture I had attended only one year earlier, I recalled that the British palaeontologist Harry Seeley had argued that the dinosaurs fell into two distinct groups, largely defined by differences in the pelvis. There were the 'bird-hipped' *Ornithischians* and the 'lizard-hipped' *Saurischians*. The exhibition had clearly been arranged along those lines.

Bradstreet appeared disinterested in the displays and got straight down to business. He asked Fulton to explain why Maddocks had deserted him at the museum when both men had been instructed to guard the building during their shift. Holmes interrupted before the perplexed sergeant could answer.

"I am sorry to interject, Inspector, but I would be keen to know what had happened prior to that. I think we need to build up a complete picture of the events earlier. We may then be in possession of all the relevant facts."

Bradstreet did not seem to be offended and merely nodded for Fulton to respond.

"We began work at ten this morning and spent the first hour at the station being briefed about the recent raids and the significance of these palaeontology collections. Stephen had no great interest in the work and was content for me to take notes and decide how best to arrange things once we got to the museum. Before making our way here he accepted my suggestion that we have a quick meal at my house. We thought it would be a long night and didn't think we'd get the chance to eat again."

"And where is it you live, Sergeant?" enquired Holmes.

"Gloucester Road, South Kensington. It's less than half a mile from here."

"I see. And what did you eat?"

The question prompted a bemused look from Bradstreet.

"I had a pie in the pantry that I'd baked the previous evening. We ate some of that with a few potatoes. I live on my own, you see, as my wife died three years back. Stephen often stayed for dinner. We've been pals since our days at the Giggleswick School near Settle."

"You both had a good education, then. Giggleswick is a public school, is it not?" I asked, somewhat surprised to hear him say this.

"Yes, Stephen's father was a barrister and could afford the fees. I received a scholarship to attend. I can't say that I enjoyed my time there, but it helped me to get this job."

Holmes then enquired, "Did you both join the Metropolitan Force at the same time?"

Fulton snorted unexpectedly. "No. I joined some years earlier than Stephen and put in a good word for him at the time he applied." He looked towards Bradstreet in a somewhat contemptable manner. "His upbringing was clearly better than mine, for he made it to *Inspector* three years ago. I've been told I'll never progress beyond *Sergeant*."

Inspector Bradstreet was not immune to the gibe. "Alright, that's enough, Fulton. Just tell us what happened after you'd had the meal."

"We walked to Cromwell Road and arrived here at about twelve-thirty. We were shown around the main exhibition area by Mr. Flower, the director of the Museum."

"William Henry Flower?" I enquired, knowing something of the man's history.

"Yes. He replaced the previous director, Sir Richard Owen. Both share a devotion to natural history although, interestingly, the two have never got on. You might remember that they fell out in various scientific circles while debating theories of evolution. Flower is a devotee of Charles Darwin, but also believes that religion and palaeontology are not incompatible." He pointed towards a white statue on one wall of the central hall. "It was he who commissioned the seated marble statue of Darwin that sits over there."

Holmes appeared to be greatly impressed by Fulton's display of knowledge. "Did Mr. Flower tell you all of this?"

"No. I take a great interest in such matters. I am something of an amateur rock collector and enjoy reading about all the new discoveries."

Bradstreet was clearly irritated by the deviation. "Can we get back to the matter at hand? What happened after you'd been *shown around* by Mr. Flower?"

"Stephen was content to wander around the hall scrutinising all of the exhibits. He seemed distracted, acting oddly, and occasionally mumbling to himself. He appeared oblivious to the fact that the building was now full of large numbers of visitors. I left him to it and began to do a tour of the museum, noting down all of the security arrangements and trying to spot the most likely areas where a break-in might occur. I suppose I might have been gone for a couple of hours. When I returned to the hall I was lambasted by an irate curator whom I had met but briefly while in the company of Mr. Flower. He said that my colleague had been causing quite a disturbance in front of the visitors and in the interests of everyone's safety he had been manhandled into the office of one of the academic staff."

Inspector Bradstreet expressed his dismay at the revelation: "Had he been drinking, Fulton?"

"No, sir. Not to my knowledge. Well, not before we came here. I found him in the company of a geologist by the name of Phelps. He had managed to calm Stephen down and was busy administering what he said was the inspector's third glass of brandy. Phelps explained that the dinosaur bones often scared some of the younger visitors, but he had never known a grown man – let alone a senior police officer – to exhibit such terror."

The word did not escape Holmes's attention. "*Terror*? Did he really say that?"

"Yes. And I soon understood why. Stephen had apparently become fixated with a fossilised Pterodactyl. The display contains a detailed drawing showing what the creature would have looked like when it was alive in the Jurassic period. He had been staring at this for some time under the watchful eye of the museum staff, before becoming convinced that the *Pterosaur* had come to life."

The narrative was too much for Bradstreet who exploded with apoplexy. "Clearly the man was intoxicated, as you know only too well, Sergeant! I have no idea what this *Ter..o..whatsit* is, but can tell you that this will not sit well with the Commissioner when he hears about it! Did you not challenge Maddocks?"

Fulton stood his ground. "I tried to talk to him, sir, but for an hour or more he spoke nothing but nonsense. For periods he would sit quietly, but would then act manically, for no particular reason, convinced that there were dinosaurs in the room with us. He kept pointing upwards, saying that he could see 'the flying reptile' and 'the Devil's own bird.'"

"And yet *you* saw nothing, so he was clearly delusional." It was more of an observation than a question. One which I then felt obliged to elaborate on: "If we accept that Maddocks had *not* been drinking before arriving at the museum, and the episodes began *before* he was ushered in Phelps's room, it is quite possible that he was experiencing some form of temporary *mania*. It is not uncommon in times of acute anxiety."

Holmes was amenable to the suggestion. "I agree, Watson. And you are right to point out that this was in all likelihood a *temporary aberration* on his part, for he displayed none of these behaviours later at 221B. And yet it seems hard to imagine that the one of the exhibits would trigger such a reaction..."

Bradstreet remained unconvinced. "Dress it up any way you wish, Mr. Holmes, but my instincts tell me he'd just had one too many. So having humiliated himself and disgraced the honour of the Yard, how did he manage to find his way to Baker Street?"

It was convenient that Bradstreet focused his attention on Fulton at that point, for both Holmes and I exchanged a look at the mention of the Yard's 'honour.'

"I sat with Stephen for a short while longer, until he began to displays signs of weariness. At that point he was laid out on a bench along one wall of Phelps's office. Convinced that he would sleep off whatever illness he was suffering from, I thought it best to leave him and continue with the work we had been asked to do.

"I went back to my earlier duties, continuing to examine all of the doors, windows and others points of access in the museum and recording these in my notebook. It was some time beyond five o'clock when I returned to the office and found it to be empty. I could not locate Phelps, learning later that he had left for the day. And enquiring about the whereabouts of my colleague, I was then told by the staff at the public entrance that Stephen had departed from the museum without saying anything and leaving no message. While concerned, I felt it was my duty to stay put as I had been instructed to do."

"Quite right," opined Bradstreet, "although you might have seen fit to send a short telegram to the station explaining what had occurred. Heaven knows how we are going to resolve this with the museum's director."

Fulton looked suitably admonished and asked if he might be relieved of his duty. There was the sound of footsteps away to our left, and I could see that the night watchman had re-entered the hall, this time in the company of two more police officers whom I imagined to be the men sent to replace Maddocks and Fulton. Inspector Bradstreet confirmed that this was indeed the case and, while releasing Fulton, made it quite clear he expected the sergeant to make a full statement of what he had told us first thing the next morning.

Holmes had been walking among the exhibits while all of this was going on and, having re-joined us, said that we would also take our leave as it had been a long day. He suggested that we might call on the inspector at one o'clock the following day. Bradstreet seemed content with this, and I confirmed that the timing would be good for me also given the planned *post mortem*. We left the main hall alongside a weary-looking Sergeant Fulton.

The temperature outside had continued to drop, although the fog had lifted somewhat making visibility that much easier. Holmes fell in with Fulton, explaining that we would walk with him as far as Gloucester Road and then try to catch a cab. I knew this to be a ruse as our route back to Baker Street was in the opposite direction, but the sergeant appeared to be none the wiser.

When we reached the left turn into Gloucester Road, Holmes announced suddenly that he felt weak and feared he might pass out. Feigning weariness and acting like he was about to collapse, he grabbed for my arm and steadied himself with his walking cane. Fulton was taken in completely, while I played along with the charade. I explained that Holmes was susceptible to such attacks when he had not eaten for some hours. The concerned sergeant said that his house was but a short walk away and he would be glad to furnish the great detective with a morsel or two to speed his recovery.

The gas lamp across the street cast a warm glow on the red-brick terraced house that Fulton occupied. It was a neatly proportioned property with a solid front door, single downstairs window and three upper windows. Stepping inside the front room it was easy to see the feminine touches of Fulton's late wife – the neatly crocheted antimacassars on the armchairs and an elaborate fabric lambrequin running along the top and sides of the window frame. It was to Fulton's credit that he had maintained the interior to an immaculate standard.

Our unwitting host invited us to make ourselves comfortable and offered to prepare some bread and cheese for our late supper.

"Splendid!" said Holmes. "That would be most agreeable. But please do not go to any particular trouble – a thin slice of bread and a small wedge of cheddar would be quite sufficient." He winked at me slyly as Fulton exited the room.

We sat in silence until the police officer returned from the kitchen, not daring to exchange any words in case we were overheard. Fulton had prepared a small plate for each of us, on which sat a sharp knife, a sizeable chunk of cheese, some pickled onions, a wholesome round of bread and a drop of homemade pickle. In spite of the obfuscation, Holmes and I enjoyed every mouthful of the repast.

With our supper consumed, Holmes insisted on collecting the empty plates and said that he would return them to the kitchen. I followed my colleague's lead and immediately engaged Fulton in conversation, asking him about the rock collection he had referred to earlier. The enquiry brought the sergeant to life as he talked effusively about his fascination with geology. Holmes returned some minutes later, a light smile playing around his lips.

We bid our farewells to Fulton, thanking him once more for the supper and making our way back out onto the street. The light fog had all but disappeared as we headed onto Cromwell Road and hailed the first empty hansom that we saw. It was only when we were seated in the cab and on our way to Baker Street that Holmes began to talk about the case.

"Fulton is our man, Watson! I felt it from the very beginning when we first approached him at the museum. I was convinced that his shocked reaction had little to do with the news about Maddocks. It was more the surprise of learning that his colleague had approached us after leaving the museum. He knows our reputation for ferreting out the truth."

I was stunned by the revelation but did not fully comprehend what he meant. "Are you saying that Fulton set out to murder Maddocks?"

"No, I don't think he did, but his actions have inadvertently led to the inspector's demise. All should become clearer when we meet with Bradstreet tomorrow at lunchtime. I have some work to complete while you are attending the autopsy with Dr. Lorrimer. We should then be a position to present our case to Scotland Yard. Maddocks did indeed see a *Pterosaur*, but like the limited vision we experienced in the fog earlier, his perception was not all it should have been.

With this cryptic allusion he fell silent and refused to be drawn further, adding only that he required "further data" to confirm his suspicions.

****

I rose early the next morning in order to attend the *post mortem* with Dr. Lorrimer. Arriving at his surgery in Harrington Road a few minutes before nine o'clock, I found he was already well advanced in his preparations for the examination. Suitably attired, I began to assist him with the dissection.

It was fascinating to see a fellow surgeon work with such dexterity. We exchanged few words at first, and I fell in with his preferred ways of operating. When he had examined all of the major organs and had begun to remove tissue samples for the toxicology tests he planned, he began to talk more freely and openly.

"Do you find it easy to work with Holmes?" he enquired, somewhat out of the blue.

I paused before responding, trying to imagine why he might have asked such a question. "I have heard others say that they find his approach somewhat brusque, but I have to say that whatever shortcomings he might possess, I have always found Holmes to be both loyal and inspirational. He is the finest man I have ever had the fortune to associate with. Why do you ask?"

The question took him by surprise. "I must apologise. I did not intend to offend you, Watson. It's just that when I'm working with some of the detectives from Scotland Yard, they seem to have few positive things to say about him. Of course, they recognise his uncanny skills and abilities, but their overwhelming view seems to be that he is a destabilising force."

"*Destabilising?!* Now there's a euphemism I can imagine coming from the likes of Bradstreet. They're content to ask for his help when all else fails. Far from being a subversive force, I would say that he helps to protect the reputation of their profession!"

Lorrimer tried to play devil's advocate. "Yes, but imagine your colleague decided to stray into your professional domain, telling you how to perform surgery or tend to your patients. You cannot tell me that you would willingly accept his *amateur interventions.*"

I could feel my hackles rising but sought to keep things civil. "There is one thing you must realise about the man, Lorrimer. He is uniquely placed to conduct the work that he does as a consulting detective. In the same way that every generation produces scientists, barristers or engineers who are at the pinnacle of their profession, Holmes is the cream of the crop when it comes to detective work. He does not claim to know everything. In fact, he is most honest about his limitations. In short, there is nothing *amateur* about his work."

To his credit, Lorrimer did not pursue the matter, realising, I suspect, that further protestations would be futile. For my part, I settled back into the routine of assisting him. Within a couple of hours we had completed the autopsy and concluded all of the tests Lorrimer felt necessary. We were agreed on the conclusions, but I could not help but think that both Bradstreet and Holmes would be disappointed with what Lorrimer had to tell them.

With the meeting at Bow Street Police Station scheduled for one o'clock, we began to clean ourselves up and ensure that we had recorded the results of all our work. Lorrimer had two mortuary assistants on standby who agreed to take over at that point, enabling us to catch a cab and arrive at the station with just a few minutes to spare.

We were shown up to the first floor of the building and into the spacious office which Inspector Bradstreet occupied. Holmes was already there, sitting to one side of Bradstreet's desk and clutching what looked look a small glass vial. He smiled at me enigmatically as I took a seat beside him.

Bradstreet welcomed us and talked through a few developments in the investigation. Sergeant Fulton had come into work earlier that morning to make a full statement. He had apologised for his actions the day before, but had requested that he be allowed to continue his patrol duties at the museum. Bradstreet had consented to the request. Beyond that, there had been no further reports of raids or thefts in the case. The inspector then invited Dr. Lorrimer to give an account of what had been discovered during the *post mortem*.

"Doctor Watson and I conducted a thorough examination and also completed a large number of laboratory tests. We confirmed that the death had been the result of an acute heart attack. However, Maddocks looked to have been in very good health and there were no obvious signs of liver, heart, lung or arterial damage which might have led to such rapid heart failure. In such a case, I would have expected to find some evidence within the blood or tissue samples of an agent which had triggered the attack. We tested for the full range of toxins which can kill with such speed – including mercury, strychnine, cyanide and arsenic – but found no traces. We then tried to ascertain the presence of other poisons, such as prussic acid, hemlock and digitalis, all without success. At this stage, we are forced to conclude that the death remains unexplained but foul play cannot be ruled out."

I nodded in agreement. Bradstreet said he was surprised to hear this and turned towards Holmes who had yet to voice any opinion. My colleague then took a curious line of questioning. "Doctor Lorrimer, did you test for any chemical deliriants?"

Lorrimer stiffened. "Meaning what, exactly?"

"I was curious to know whether you had tested for any chemicals which might have induced Maddocks to see an extinct flying reptile at the museum yesterday. It was, after all, the most singular and fascinating aspect of this whole affair."

The surgeon bristled even more. "Maddocks was clearly delusional and I must say that I tend to agree with Inspector Bradstreet that his condition was most likely the result of too much alcohol."

Holmes was polite, but direct. "I cannot agree, as I believe it was only after seeing the *Pterosaur* that Maddocks began to drink. It is well known that certain chemicals can trigger hallucinations, perceptual anomalies and other substantial subjective changes in human thoughts, emotions, and consciousness. I believe that someone administered such a deliriant deliberately."

It was Bradstreet's turn to raise a query: "To kill Maddocks?!"

"No. To put him into a delusional state in which his judgement – and ability to do his job – would be hampered.

The inspector confessed to being more than a little confused. "Mr. Holmes. As entertaining as your theories often are, I find myself at a loss with this one. Can you get to the point and explain exactly what it is you are asserting?"

"Certainly, Inspector. Sergeant Fulton set out to undermine Maddocks's position as the senior officer on this case. I cannot be certain, but imagine he has held a deep-seated hatred for Maddocks since his colleague was promoted to inspector and he was overlooked for promotion. The fact that all of this occurred at the same time as Fulton lost his beloved wife is probably a contributory factor. I met Fulton for the first time some three months back in the company of Maddocks. It was clear to me then that he had an intense dislike of the other man and was trying very hard to conceal it. I noted the fact at the time, but did not imagine it would ever prove to be relevant in a criminal case. Eager to learn more about their so-called friendship, I sent a telegram to the Giggleswick School this morning. The headmaster replied, saying that he remembered both boys and confirmed that they were fiercely competitive, often coming to blows, with Fulton almost always the underdog."

Bradstreet looked at him askance. "The pair could be bull-headed certainly, but I find this hard to believe. How exactly did he put Maddocks in this *delusional state* and, more importantly, what reason did he have for going to such extraordinary lengths?"

Holmes nodded. "Let me answer the first of those questions, as it will set the scene for the second. I have known Maddocks for some time and always believed him to be a sober, level-headed man not given to flights of fancy. His practical, hard-nosed approach to policing had much to commend it. Now, he said he saw an extinct reptile and ordinarily I would be inclined to take his account at face value. And yet clearly such a sighting would be improbable unless he had truly discovered a lost world*.

"Having heard Fulton's testimony, I was convinced that Maddocks had seen what he believed to be a flying reptile. Now, had he been completely delusional, the symptoms would have manifested themselves sometime earlier and would have persisted later when he arrived at Baker Street. I concluded therefore, that he must have ingested something just before the walk to the museum which prompted these temporary hallucinations. And it was Fulton's account which gave me the first clue. You may remember that he said they'd eaten *a pie* which he had baked the previous evening.

"Watson and I walked with Fulton to his home when he left the museum last night. It was a deliberate tactic on my part. We had some supper with him and, just before I left the house, I was able to gain access to the pantry without the man's knowledge. There was evidence in the kitchen that he and Maddocks had eaten a meal exactly as he had suggested. I would have expected nothing less, for there had been no opportunity to clear up as the pair had gone straight to the museum after their lunch. And yet, I discovered that he had been somewhat economical with the truth when he said he had baked *a pie*. In fact, there were the remains of *two pies* in the pantry. One had been baked especially for Maddocks."

Dr. Lorrimer huffed. "How could you know that?"

Holmes smiled and raised the glass vial. "Because of this. I took samples from both pies and tested them myself this morning. Both contained a variety of edible fungi, but one contained a recognisable deliriant. A bucket in the pantry also contained some of the discarded remains of the mushrooms used in the pies. Having gathered some of those as well, I was able to identify the fungus responsible for Maddocks's condition. The distinctive brown, conical-shaped mushroom is known as the 'liberty cap'. The German mycologist Paul Kummer gave it the scientific name of *Psilocybe semilanceata* in 1871."

I recollected an article in *The Lancet* some years earlier which had detailed an account of poisoning by liberty cap mushrooms. In 1799, a family picked some of the fungus in London's Green Park and ate them in a meal. It was documented that the father and children had experienced pupil dilation, delirium and uncontrollable laughter. I knew that Holmes had hit upon the agent responsible for the officer's malaise. Lorrimer, however, remained unconvinced.

"I'm aware that liberty cap mushrooms can induce hallucinations, but have never known them to cause death."

Holmes's jaw was set hard. "I did not suggest that the fungus killed him, merely that it gave rise to the mental state in which he was able to see a living creature which has been extinct for some considerable time."

Bradstreet intervened. "I think you may be on to something there, Mr. Holmes. I have known Fulton to talk about his forays into the countryside to collect mushrooms and the like. He's very knowledgeable about the natural world. In fact, he asked to work with Maddocks on this investigation because of his interest in old rocks and bones."

"That is most telling."

"In what sense?"

"Because Fulton had a material interest in being *on the inside* of this investigation. In fact, it is the reason he has gone to the *extraordinary lengths* you enquired about earlier. He has been supplying information to the gang responsible for all of the recent raids and break-ins. That is why he worked so diligently to assess the security arrangements at the museum. The information will be used by his criminal associates who plan to raid the dinosaur collection this very evening."

I was astonished to learn this. Bradstreet also appeared stunned. Even Lorrimer looked as if he had been knocked off his perch.

"How do you know all of this?" Bradstreet asked.

"Observation, deduction and legwork," replied Holmes, "the essence of our craft. It was clear from Fulton's talk at the museum that he knows a great deal about palaeontology – the casual references to 'Ichthyosaur', 'Jurassic period' and *'Pterosaur'*. He is also likely to know which exhibits are the rarest and most likely to fetch the highest price when sold illegally to fossil collectors around the world.

"When we first entered the exhibition hall Fulton looked shocked. This was not because he had learned of Maddocks's death, but because he realised that Watson and I had been visited by his colleague. How could he be sure that Maddocks had not become aware of his scheme to deceive everyone? So he played it cautiously, emphasising Maddocks's bizarre behaviour as a smokescreen for what he was really been up to.

"When we greeted Fulton, Dr. Watson and I shook him by the hand. I noted that he had a chalky residue on the tips of his fingers. There had to be a reason. Taking the time to wander among the exhibits, I observed the explanation. Visibly, but discreetly, Fulton had chalked a small 'M' on the floor to the side of a number of the displays. A direction to the thieves, showing which fossils should be stolen."

"Why 'M'?" interrupted Lorrimer.

"A recognised gang symbol or somebody's initial, I suspect. In any case, he had done a very comprehensive job of working out how best to get in and out of the museum without the need to spend time deciding which fossils to steal."

I cut in. "I see. And feeding Maddocks the mushrooms was a ruse to keep him out of the way, while Fulton did his work."

"Exactly. Maddocks was a solid detective, who would have known that his colleague was up to something. And the more Maddocks acted strangely, the more he was likely to distract the museum workers and visitors from what Fulton was doing. That would also explain why Fulton was in no hurry to let the station know of Maddocks's condition, just in case further officers arrived to stop him completing his reconnaissance."

"Why are you so sure that this break-in will be tonight?" asked Bradstreet, reaching for a cigarette from a small wooden box to the side of the desk. He offered the box around although no one took up the offer.

"This is where the legwork came in," Holmes responded. "Having returned to Baker Street last night, I was convinced that Fulton was working with the criminals behind the fossil raids. Even at that late hour, I was able to despatch some trusted associates of my own to watch Fulton's house. I have a small band of loyal street urchins who are willing to carry out such work. Just before I set off to come here today, I received word from Wiggins, their designated leader. Fulton had left Gloucester Road at around five o'clock this morning, heading into the city. One of my young allies by the name of Remblance was able to follow the sergeant at a safe distance.

"Fulton's destination was a brewer's yard close to Brick Lane. Remblance was able to slip into the yard unseen. Following the sound of two voices, he positioned himself behind some barrels and heard most of the conversation which followed. The excellent information he was later to relay to Wiggins has earned the boys a guinea prize.

"In short, Fulton confirmed that the break-in is set for eight o'clock this evening. A stolen key will enable the raiders to gain entry through a large oak door at the back of the museum. Six men will be involved, travelling to the raid aboard a brewery dray containing large oak barrels and long wooden boxes. From their conversation, Remblance formed the impression that the gang had used this method to steal fossils on previous occasions. He heard Fulton say that only one night watchman will be on duty and that he would be 'taken care of, by eight o'clock.' When the raiders have lifted all of the marked exhibits, they will rough Fulton up and leave him bound and gagged on the floor of the museum to give every impression that he was overwhelmed by the gang."

"Extraordinary!" roared Bradstreet. "That is a remarkable piece of detective work, Mr. Holmes. And it is some credit to your young accomplices that they have been so adept at outwitting Fulton, who is clearly no fool. This duplicity by one of our own will not go down well with the commissioner, but if we can intervene early, prevent the night watchman from being hurt, and catch these thieves red-handed, I believe we should be able to snatch victory from the jaws of defeat!"

I had never known Bradstreet to be so complimentary. We had first encountered the inspector in 1882 on a case I had recorded as *The Manila Envelope*. At that stage he was serving in Scotland Yard's 'E' Division and still retained some enthusiasm for the role. Seven years later, he had been transferred to "B' Division to serve out his remaining years as a detective. From what I had gathered, it had not been a move he had welcomed.

There was little more to discuss at that stage. Bradstreet thanked Dr. Lorrimer for his work and asked him if he would work with the local coroner in enabling the inquest into Maddocks's death to be completed. The doctor confirmed that he would, but expressed some concern about the likely verdict given what we now knew about the liberty cap mushrooms. In reply, Bradstreet said that he also thought it unlikely that Fulton would face a charge of either 'murder' or 'attempted murder' for what he had done.

To that point, I had imagined that Holmes would want to be in on the subsequent arrest and detention of Fulton and the fossil thieves. Bradstreet also seemed surprised when my colleague announced that he was content to let Scotland Yard conclude the business and was not seeking any recognition for our involvement in the case. I wanted to voice my objection, but knew that Holmes would not welcome such a challenge in front of the others.

It was only when we were sat before a warm fire in the cosy surrounds of the Baker Street apartment that he shared his real reason for not wishing to see the case through.

"There are times, Watson, when it is better to leave Scotland Yard in ignorance of certain facts. It seems quite clear to me that in the rush to bring Fulton to justice and the eagerness to thwart a gang of high-profile fossil thieves, the death of poor Maddocks has been largely obscured. Lorrimer was not wrong to suggest that the deliriant mushrooms were unlikely to have been the cause of his demise. You see I took a walk through Green Park this morning before making my way to Bow Street. It is only two miles from Fulton's house. I found liberty cap mushrooms growing in abundance, alongside all of the other fungi that had been baked in the pie fed to Maddocks."

"Is that not a confirmation of everything you expected?" I asked, unsure where he was heading with his narrative.

"Indeed. But it was only when I chanced upon some of the browny-grey edible mushrooms that I had also seen in Fulton's pantry, that I realised what had killed Maddocks. The common ink cap was first recorded by the French naturalist Pierre Bulliard in 1786. He named it *Agaricus atramentarious* from the Latin *atramentum* meaning 'ink'. In the middle ages, the fungus had been used to produce a cheap supply of the writing fluid. While palatable, the mushroom has an unusual property. When mixed with alcohol it produces a toxin which can lead to symptoms such as flushing, malaise, agitation, palpitations..."

"...and occasionally, heart failure!" I exclaimed. "That's it, Holmes! At the museum, Phelps had already and unknowingly plied Maddocks with at least three glasses of brandy to calm him down. When he arrived here he downed a further large glass, increasing the intensity of the poison. It was the spirits that killed him, rather than the sight of the Pterodactyl!"

Holmes nodded. "Yes, and you might know that the traditional name of the ink cap is 'Tippler's Bane'.

****

It was some months before Sergeant Fulton was to face trial alongside a dozen of his criminal associates. The gang had been responsible for fossil thefts across length and breadth of Europe, selling the scientific rarities to collectors for sizeable sums of money. Most of the men received sentences of between seven and fifteen years. But the judicial system reserved the largest sentence for the corrupt police officer – Fulton being incarcerated for a minimum of twenty years.

Bradstreet's only disappointment was Scotland Yard's failure to detain the one person who had apparently orchestrated the enterprise. All of the convicted men received their sentences without divulging his name or whereabouts. They referred to him simply as 'M.'

Holmes rarely talked about the case in the years that followed. When he did, it was often with a faraway look in his eye which accompanied the words: "Like the spectral *Pterosaur*, we will all be extinct one day."

*Note: Readers may be aware that my literary agent, Sir Arthur Conan Doyle, is credited with having written a wholly fictional account of just such a world. – JHW.

7. The Conk-Singleton Forgery Case

The highly obsessive collector can be a danger both to himself and to all of those who would stand in the way of his compulsive personality. Place a rare or desirable artefact within his grasp and he will go to extraordinary lengths to own it. Tempt him with the unique or definitive piece and he may risk life or limb to satisfy his desires. That Arthur Conk-Singleton was an obsessive collector was clear to all who knew him. What was not so clear was whether his acquisitiveness had led to his death.

It was in the spring of 1900 that Holmes was first invited to assist Scotland Yard in the murder investigation. Arthur Conk-Singleton was a wealthy retired banker who appeared to be fanatical about money in all its forms. The fifty-eight year old bachelor had filled his South Kensington home with a rare and prized collection. No fewer than seven of his well-proportioned rooms had been fitted out with large display cabinets containing banknotes, coins and promissory notes from all parts of the world. The collection contained some of the earliest and most sought-after examples of paper money, produced in China during the Tang and Song dynasties of the 7th century. His more recent acquisitions included banknotes and coins issued by the unified territories of Italy and Germany. In fact, there was no currency that the man had overlooked in his quest to build the ultimate collection.

As a trustee of the Numismatic Society of London, Conk-Singleton was, by all accounts, a well-regarded, but inherently secretive collector. Only a handful of his colleagues had ever been invited to the house; fewer still had been shown around the entire collection. He had only one known relative – a bedbound older brother, Francis, who lived in Eastbourne and claimed to have had little time for his sibling, and even less interest in Arthur's hobby. As a devout Anglican, Francis held to the age-old maxim that *money is the root of all evil.* And while shocked to hear of the murder, he said it came as no surprise, explaining to the police that Arthur had cultivated few real friendships in life and seemed content to make an enemy of anyone who stood between him and his next acquisition.

The sequence of events leading to the murder seemed straightforward enough. In the early evening of Sunday, 13th May, Conk-Singleton had received a visitor. He had been alone in the house at the time, his elderly housekeeper being in the habit of attending an evening church service at nearby St. Stephen's. That he had known the caller was clear from the evidence in the parlour. Conk-Singleton had poured two glasses of expensive Madeira, which had then been consumed – the empty glasses and bottle were still sitting where they had been placed on a small oval table between two comfortable armchairs. At some point thereafter, the two had made their way from the parlour into the largest of the rooms in which the currency collection was housed. It was here that the body had been found. Conk-Singleton had been shot once through the back at close range by a small handgun. The wound had been sufficient to kill him relatively quickly. Having been absent for less than two hours, the housekeeper had returned to the house around eight-thirty to find her employer dead.

It was late in the afternoon on the day after the murder when Inspector Lestrade called in at 221B. At that time, we had become used to his social calls and the news that he often brought from Scotland Yard. Sometimes he would share the particulars of one case or another, and Holmes would do his best to point the capable detective in the right direction. On this particular occasion our friend seemed most subdued and Holmes was quick to encourage him to tell us what troubled him.

"An odd case, Mr. Holmes – one that should be straightforward, but is proving to be anything but."

My colleague leaned forward in his chair, offering Lestrade a ready-made cigarette from his silver case and passing across an ashtray. "Then you must tell us all about it!"

Lestrade outlined the key facts of the case as I have already set them before you. In the twenty-four hours since being called to South Kensington, his officers had conducted extensive enquiries, interviewing the housekeeper, nearby neighbours, officials at the Numismatic Society of London and the brother in Eastbourne. While they now knew more about the victim and the manner of his death, the motive for the killing remained a mystery. A single bullet had been removed from the man's heart during the *post mortem*. It had come from the barrel of a Colt Derringer .41 calibre rim fire pistol. No one had been seen entering or leaving the house and no shot had been heard by any of those living close to the ex-banker.

Holmes and I listened intently. When Lestrade paused, I asked, "Could the motive have been robbery?"

"No, doctor. As far as we can determine, nothing has been taken. The housekeeper is a woman of meticulous habits. She has been with her employer for more than twenty years and knows every square inch of the property. She says that she can see nothing out of place."

"Then perhaps the robbery was foiled. Could it have been the return of the housekeeper that prompted the culprit to flee?"

"Again, we do not believe that to be the case. The house has only two doors, front and rear. Both were locked when the housekeeper returned, she having her own set of keys. The key to the back door was still in the lock, so the killer could not have left that way. Mr. Conk-Singleton was as fanatical about security as he was with his collection. All of the windows have locks and each was secure when we arrived. The front door must have been the point of exit, for the locking mechanism can be sprung from the inside, but is reset as soon as the door is shut. Had the killer left when the housekeeper arrived, they would have passed on the threshold. Beyond that, I see it as no coincidence that our assailant arrived when the housekeeper was absent. I believe he planned it that way, knowing she would be out."

Holmes then spoke. "That is possible, but by no means certain. Now, tell us more about this society that our man belonged to. Are you thinking that the killer may have been a member?"

Lestrade nodded, adding, "Since retiring from the bank two years ago, Conk-Singleton has lived as something of a recluse. The housekeeper said that he only ever left home to visit auctions and attend the bi-monthly meetings of the Numismatic Society. The infrequent visitors he received were all fellow collectors."

"Then your working hypothesis would seem to be a fair one, Lestrade. How many trustees and members are there in the society?"

"Forty-four, of which seven are known to have previously called on Conk-Singleton."

"Then your list of suspects is not extensive."

"No, but it is problematic."

"How so?"

"Each man has a solid alibi for where he was at the time of the murder."

"I see. And you have no other leads?"

Lestrade took a final draw on his cigarette, before stubbing it out in the ashtray beside him. "No."

"So how did you leave the scene of the crime? I hope you have not allowed the *meticulous* housekeeper to destroy any evidence that might remain?"

Lestrade snickered. "Mr. Holmes, I know your methods well enough! I have a constable at the property with strict instructions to let no one in without my say so. The housekeeper has been persuaded to move out for a couple of days and is currently staying with her sister in Nuneaton. Naturally, I was hoping that you might find time to travel across to South Kensington to see if we have missed anything."

My colleague gave him the broadest of smiles. "Your faith is well-placed, my friend. Watson and I would be delighted to assist. And there is no time like the present!"

****

It took us little time to travel by carriage to the handsome Italianate townhouse on Gloucester Road. We were greeted at the door by a young constable who looked visibly relieved when Inspector Lestrade announced that there was no further need for him to remain on guard at the property.

Holmes was eager to learn what he could and with his magnifying glass to hand asked Lestrade to direct him immediately towards the parlour. The room he entered was spacious with a high ceiling and ornate chandelier. The décor was distinctly masculine – the curtains, wallpaper and furnishings being dark green and giving the room a sombre almost funereal feel. To the left side of the room I could see the small oval table and armchairs where the Madeira had been poured. Close by was a large mahogany chest on which sat a Tantalus, an assortment of glasses and a dozen or more bottles of fortified wine.

Holmes approached the table slowly, taking in all aspects of the scene before him, and scrutinising the carpet beneath the table and the seat of one of the chairs. With a small pair of tweezers he picked at the chair a couple of times removing some tiny fragments which he placed in an envelope he had withdrawn from a pocket. Lestrade and I knew better than to interrupt him as he went about his work.

He then turned his attention to the table top itself. Having run the magnifying glass over the glasses and bottle, he announced suddenly: "You were not wrong, Lestrade. This exquisite Bual Madeira was produced by Blandy's and does not come cheap. And yet, Conk-Singleton's other wines tell me that he was certainly no connoisseur. Perhaps this had been a gift to him or a one-off purchase. Either way, I would suggest that he opened this particular bottle in order to impress his visitor. And impressed she seems to have been, for the glass is completely drained."

Lestrade's face lit up. "The visitor was a woman?"

"Without doubt. There were two long dark hairs on the seat of the chair. I would venture that these were not left by the elderly housekeeper. The visitor used a gloved hand to wipe the lipstick from her glass, but has left one tiny – but telling – smudge near the rim. The lipstick is unusual. It was manufactured by Guerlain, the French cosmetic company. I know this because I have made a particular study of popular cosmetics and hope one day to complete a monograph on the subject."

"Then our killer is indeed a bold one, Mr. Holmes."

"Yes. And I think we can take it that the timing of her visit was suggested by Mr. Conk-Singleton."

"Why do you say that?" I asked.

"Because he knew that his housekeeper would be absent at that time. I am sure that our ex-bank manager would not want it known that he had been entertaining a lady caller in his parlour on a Sunday evening. That much is speculation on my part. It remains to be seen whether it is borne out by the facts."

With nothing further of note in the parlour, we made our way to the large room in which Conk-Singleton's body had been found. Lestrade's men had positioned a thin line of white cord to indicate where the body had been. Holmes seemed impressed by the initiative they had shown. He then focused on the murder weapon. "The Colt Derringer was an ideal pistol for our killer – lightweight, easy to operate and small enough to be concealed within a handbag. At close range, it required no great expertise. The report from the gun would have been relatively quiet, helping to explain why none of the neighbours heard the shot. In any case, this room sits within the centre of the house, well away from the boundaries of the property."

He began to examine the cabinet closest to where the body had fallen, his magnifying glass being used to scan the area around the locks and handles of the two doors of the glass-fronted case. The ceiling in this room was significantly lower than that of the parlour and the cabinet stood at a height of about seven feet. Inside was arranged a display of American banknotes, all clipped expertly into position, each with its own printed caption beneath, detailing dates of issue and other pertinent information.

"The cabinet is unlocked, Lestrade. There are fingerprints on both the glass and the handles of the doors, which I suspect are Conk-Singleton's. Had you not noticed?"

The man from Scotland Yard stepped closer to the case and followed Holmes's outstretched finger. "Well, I never! No, I didn't think to check as I could see that none of the banknotes was missing. Do you think that's significant?"

"Yes. It lends weight to Watson's theory that the motive may have been robbery. It could be that our lady killer shot Conk-Singleton in order to steal one of these banknotes and replace it with a duplicate."

"Like a forgery, you mean?"

"Possibly." Holmes opened the doors to the display case and stepped closer. Through the lens of the magnifying glass he began to examine each of the banknotes in turn and then began to chuckle. "Now it is my turn to be surprised. While I am no expert in American currency, I would say that all of these particular notes have one thing in common."

"Which is?"

"They are all forgeries – for this is a display of counterfeit notes. And beautifully executed they are too, with the exception of this one." His hand had extended towards a twenty dollar bill which sat at eye level in the centre of the display, labelled '*E Ninger, 1885*'. "Compared to the others, this is a crude piece of work – a banknote printed from a poor quality engraved plate. Note how indistinct the representation of the eagle is. An accomplished counterfeiter would never be content with such work."

I had to confess to being confused. "Holmes, are you saying that this woman killed Conk-Singleton in order to steal a counterfeit note, and merely replace it with another forgery? I can see no sense in that."

"As strange as it might seem, I do believe that to be the case. We clearly have more ground to unearth. Now, let us examine the other display cabinets."

It took us a good hour to complete the tour of the entire collection housed within the seven rooms. At the conclusion of this we had learnt one further significant fact. The vast majority of Conk Singleton's collection was made up of genuine banknotes and coins from across the globe. But he had set aside one room for an unusual collection of American counterfeits – the very room in which he had been murdered.

Standing once again within the room, Lestrade asked: "Why do you think he collected only American counterfeits?"

My colleague took a short while to answer. "A very astute question. While I cannot be sure at this stage, I would say that our man collected only the most prized and valuable of banknotes and coins. Nothing we have seen today looks commonplace. The two most forged currencies in recent decades have been the US dollar and the British pound. Both hold a value beyond their own shores and are therefore copied across the world. But collecting the very best counterfeits is problematic. While poorly forged currency does not stay in circulation long – and is readily destroyed by any bank that discovers it – a well-executed counterfeit may remain undetected for some considerable time. When these are uncovered, the authorities will often retain and study them in order to identify the engraver at the heart of the criminal enterprise. Tracking down the pushers and passers of forged banknotes is not difficult, getting to the counterfeiter often is."

I was still confused. "So you are saying that the supply of counterfeits is limited, for when they are detected they are either destroyed or put under lock and key by the banking authorities."

It was Lestrade who answered. "Yes, Doctor. And the supply is even more restricted in this country, for it is illegal to be in possession of a forged note. All counterfeit currency must be turned over to the Bank of England."

To which, Holmes added: "Precisely. Conk-Singleton faced no restrictions in collecting American forgeries, but would have been acting outside the law in accumulating British counterfeits."

My bemusement continued. "That may help to explain why he collected only American banknotes, but I still do not understand why he wanted to acquire forgeries in the first place, when they have no monetary value. Surely, of itself, a forgery is worthless."

Holmes chortled. "In most cases, yes. But you are missing the point. These well-executed counterfeits are often seen by collectors as *works of art*. And in short supply, their value can soar way beyond the face value of the currency they imitate." He pointed once more at the display case. "This collection covers what I believe is often referred to as the 'Golden Age of Counterfeiting' – the thirty-year period to 1896 when the most accomplished American forgers made their mark and operated with relative impunity in the face of attempts by the US Secret Service to shut them down. For example, this hundred-dollar bill is the work of Charles F Ulrich, a Prussian by birth. Having made the passage to the US in the 1850s, he produced engraved plates for some of the finest counterfeits the world has ever seen. This specimen could fetch as much as two thousand dollars at auction. I suspect that Conk-Singleton's entire collection is literally worth a fortune."

"Then why did our thief and murderess not take the other forgeries?" said I.

"That," replied Holmes, "is our key line of enquiry. For therein lies the answer to this mystery. Why indeed?"

We spent a further half-hour searching through Conk-Singleton's personal correspondence. It was Lestrade who eventually uncovered the crucial piece of information; a ledger book detailing every item housed in the South Kensington collection. It demonstrated that Conk-Singleton had been collecting for a good thirty years, but had been accumulating items in greater numbers since retiring two years before. Every entry in the book showed what had been acquired – the date of its purchase, the name of the seller or auction house and the price paid. We spent some time looking over the section on American counterfeits, trying to find each corresponding item in the display case before us. What it revealed did not answer our primary question, but did highlight another anomaly. The twenty-dollar *'E Ninger'* exhibit, which Holmes believed had been stolen and replaced, had been obtained from an *'Edward Marr'* on the *'16th August 1896.'* Unlike every other item listed in the ledger, it had no recorded purchase price. Where there should have been a written value, Conk-Singleton had merely added a dash.

"Curious," said Holmes. "Perhaps he was given the banknote or exchanged it for something else. He may even have stolen it. I am sure that all will become clearer when we have located our mystery woman."

"And how do you plan to do that, Mr. Holmes?"

"My dear Lestrade. You must leave this matter with us, for there is still some legwork to be done. It may be weeks, rather than days, before I am in possession of all the pertinent facts, but feel confident that we can eventually wrap up this little conundrum for you."

A look of joy swept across the inspector's ferret-like face. "That is extremely kind. I am very grateful to you both."

****

Holmes's assessment proved to be accurate, for it was indeed some weeks before we were able to bring the matter to a close. In the days following our visit to South Kensington, he made a dozen or more trips to the telegraph office, despatching telegrams to some of his contacts in America and reading through his collection of 'Counterfeit Detector' booklets, which had been produced by John S Dye, the US Treasury expert. Every new piece of information seemed to invigorate him.

Inspector Lestrade continued to visit us and it was during this same period that Holmes assisted him with *The Adventure of the Six Napoleons*. But on the matter of the Conk-Singleton forgery case, Holmes refused to be drawn until he had completed his investigation.

The final conclusion came unexpectedly. Holmes had been reading through some papers that had arrived by post that particular morning. He turned to me and announced: "Watson, I have been a fool! Thus far, I have determined why Conk-Singleton was able to obtain the Ninger counterfeit and the reason he was so keen to own it. I also know all about the man he obtained it from. Yet none of this got me any closer to our killer. In fact, I had begun to fear that this illusive femme fatale might remain hidden. It is only now that I realise just how slow I have been to consider *how* Conk-Singleton knew her and the reason she was invited to his home. To this point, I had imagined their coming together was the result of a sordid romantic affair, driven by the desires of the unmarried ex-banker. How wrong I was!

"I asked the Numismatic Society of London to send me details of all their members. These papers arrived earlier. I fear that I have been blinded by my own chauvinism. A perusal of the information reveals that the society currently has two *female* members. One is an eighty-six year old widow from East Grinstead, who has taken over the membership of her late husband. The other is a '*Mrs. Jean Carrington*,' a thirty-eight year old American who currently resides in Southwark. Alongside an obvious fascination with currency collecting, she lists her wider interests as 'painting, sculpture and plate engraving'!"

"Good heavens!" said I. "Sounds like the profile of a counterfeiter!"

"Exactly – it is too much of a coincidence. I suggest we arrange to meet up with Inspector Lestrade and pay a visit to this Mrs. Carrington. On the way I will brief you both about what I have discovered to date. Let us hope that she can complete our understanding of the Conk-Singleton case!"

Having received from Lestrade a reply to our earlier telegram, we arranged for a four-wheeler to take us to Bow Street Police Station where the doughty inspector agreed to meet us for the trip to Southwark.

The afternoon was exceptionally warm and sunny and Lestrade's forehead glistened with perspiration as he climbed into the carriage and hastily removed his jacket. Dispensing with the pleasantries, Holmes began to tell Lestrade about

Mrs. Carrington and outlined the facts of the case as the carriage headed south of the city.

"It seems you were a little economical with the background information on Arthur Conk-Singleton, Lestrade. While you mentioned that he had recently retired from a 'city bank,' he had actually been in a senior position within the Bank of England itself. In fact, he was responsible for investigating the activities of counterfeiters. In this role, he was called to look into the affairs of a seventy-year-old American forger by the name of Edward Marr, who had been caught in possession of two engraved plates and a printing press used to produce some illicit five pound notes that had gone into circulation in the early part of 1896.

"Edward Marr was extremely fearful about the position he found himself in, having a number of previous convictions for 'shoving,' or passing counterfeit money. He knew that if the bank could prove him to be the engraver of the forged plates, he was likely to spend the rest of his natural life in prison. Conk-Singleton had a reputation for being tough on those he investigated and ruthless when it came to recommending the charges the police should bring against suspects. So imagine the surprise within the bank when he announced in the August of that year, at the end of his month-long investigation, that Marr should face only the charge of passing counterfeit money, as there was no evidence that he had actually engraved the plates. The bank had little choice but to accept his conclusions, but suspected that some conspiracy had been involved. In short, it was this episode that led to him being 'persuaded' to take early retirement from the bank."

Lestrade was quick to see the significance of what he had heard. "So it is not far-fetched to imagine that Conk-Singleton and Marr struck a deal. Perhaps the pair got to know each other during the investigation and Conk-Singleton let it slip that he collected American counterfeits. Marr then says he can lay his hands on a rare forged note, but only in return for the investigator's help in reducing his likely sentence..."

Holmes beamed. "My thoughts exactly!" If you remember the date in the ledger, he obtained the Ninger counterfeit on the 16th August – the day before he concluded his investigation into Edward Marr."

"So what happened to the forger?" I asked.

"Marr was sentenced to seven years in Wandsworth Prison, where he would end his days. Eighteen months into his sentence he was stabbed to death. The authorities were unable to determine who had murdered him, but the prison governor concluded that the death had been an execution. Marr was well-connected in London and New York and knew all of the principal counterfeiters operating in both cities. Shortly before his death he had approached the governor offering to trade information on his former associates in return for a commutation of his sentence. It seems that someone was eager to prevent that from happening."

Lestrade was perched on the edge of his seat listening attentively to every word. "This Mrs. Carrington must have some connection to Marr. Could it be his daughter?"

"That is my working hypothesis, given her age, nationality and interests. 'Carrington' would be her married name."

"And the murder is revenge for what Conk-Singleton had done to her father?"

"More likely revenge for what he *didn't do* for her father. He clearly helped to reduce the charges brought against the forger, but at the end of the day Marr still received a seven-year sentence. If he could not shorten his term, he knew he was likely to die in prison. He therefore took the risky step of approaching the prison governor with the offer of information."

I still had a nagging concern about one feature of the case. "If you are correct, that would explain why Mrs. Carrington was driven to kill Conk-Singleton. But why did she go to the trouble of replacing the Ninger counterfeit? In exacting her revenge, she could have stolen the entire collection of counterfeit notes, especially if they are as valuable as you suggested some weeks back."

"A good point, Watson, and a very telling one. The Ninger counterfeit had been her father's and is extremely valuable. It was the only banknote in Conk-Singleton's collection that could tie her to the crime. She could not leave it behind, but clearly did not want anyone to know it had been replaced. And it was a subterfuge that nearly worked, for both the housekeeper and our friend Lestrade here were unaware that anything had been taken from the display cabinet."

Lestrade smiled weakly, but added. "She must have planned it that way, for she clearly had with her another forged note to replace it."

"Precisely so, and I think it highly likely that the note she replaced it with was one that she had produced herself."

"As a counterfeiter!"

"You've got it. No doubt she was encouraged by her father to learn plate engraving from an early age."

By this stage our carriage was heading along Borough High Street close to the Marshalsea Prison. The streets and pavements were crowded with all manner of street vendors, idlers and loiterers. It was but a short distance to our destination.

"Why is this Ninger counterfeit so sought after?" I asked.

Holmes grinned and it was clear that he had been waiting for the moment when he could tell this part of the story. He savoured every part of the narrative that followed.

"You may remember, a year or so ago, I had occasion to assist William P. Hazen, chief of the New York bureau of the Secret Service, with the arrest of two would-be assassins. When their plot to kill President McKinley had been thwarted, the pair fled to London hoping to escape justice. I was able to track them down to their hideout in Bermondsey. They were eventually extradited to the United States. Hazen was extremely grateful for my assistance and we have maintained a regular contact ever since.

"The Secret Service has two distinct, yet unconnected duties. Firstly, it operates to protect the presidency. But it is also the agency charged with preventing and detecting all forms of domestic currency counterfeiting. Hazen was only too pleased to respond to my various telegrams and provide information on both Edward Marr and the enigmatic Ninger. As it transpired, he is very well-acquainted with the latter.

"Emanuel Ninger is a well-built, blue-eyed man with a sandy-coloured beard. He arrived in the United States with his wife, Adele, in December 1882, having travelled by steamship from the Dutch port of Rotterdam. Then aged thirty-five, Ninger was principally a sign painter, although his initial choice of profession brought in little money. The couple settled first in Hoboken, but using some money Adele had inherited from her first marriage, decided to buy a farm in Westfield, New Jersey. It was here that Ninger began to produce the counterfeit notes he has become infamous for.

"Unlike most forgers, who engrave the copper plates from which counterfeit banknotes can be printed, Ninger is a pen and ink counterfeiter, at one time dubbed 'Jim the Penman.' He would obtain fine quality bond paper from the same mill as that used by the US Treasury's Bureau of Engraving & Printing to produce genuine banknotes. He then cut the paper to size and soaked the rectangles in a weak solution of coffee, giving them the appearance of age. While still wet, he placed the bond paper over the face of a genuine note and carefully aligned the two on a pane of glass. As the bond paper would be very nearly translucent, he was then able to see every feature of the legal tender, which he could trace onto the bond paper using a hard lead pencil. When the paper was completely dry, he would set about the delicate and time-consuming task of copying the detail of the original banknote using pen and ink, and adding colour with the application of a camel hair brush.

"For over ten years, Ninger produced his exquisitely hand-drawn banknotes and passed the bills himself on monthly trips to Manhattan. In that time, he may have produced as much as $40,000 worth of bogus currency. One curious feature of his work was the omission of the credit line: 'Engraved and Printed at the Bureau of Engraving & Printing.' It was almost as if he did not want anyone else to take the credit for his artistry.

"Of course, the enterprise could not continue as it did forever and, on a fateful trip to New York in March 1896, he was arrested for trying to pass a fifty-dollar counterfeit in a saloon. In May of that year he was sentenced to serve six years in the Erie County Penitentiary. Since that time, Ninger's rare counterfeits have continued to gain in value, being eagerly sought by collectors across the world. Ironically, they are highly-prized by other forgers, who recognise that they have more than just street value. Chief Hazen was not in the least surprised to learn that Edward Marr, a former resident of Manhattan, should have been in possession of one of Ninger's finest twenty-dollar bills."

"That is truly remarkable!" cried Lestrade, shaking his head in astonishment.

"I agree. Now, let us see what Mrs. Carrington has to say for herself. If I am not mistaken, we have just arrived at her address on Lant Street.

We stepped down from the carriage a few doors along from the house in question. Holmes paid the driver and asked him to wait for a short while in case we found no one at home.

The property sat in the middle of a block of three small, but neatly proportioned, two-storey houses. Standing before the red-painted entrance, Holmes rapped on the door with his walking cane. The sound echoed down the hallway of the house. Presently, we heard a key being turned in the lock and when the door opened there stood before us a slim, elegant woman with a mass of long dark hair. Her penetrating blue eyes flickered quickly across our faces, but she retained a confident-looking composure.

"Mrs. Jean Carrington?" asked Holmes.

"Yes. Have you come about this month's rent? I have told the landlord that I will have it for him by Friday of this week." Her New York accent was unmistakable.

"No," replied my colleague. "We are here about a more serious matter. My name is Sherlock Holmes and this is my colleague, Dr. Watson." Pointing to his right, he then added, "And this is Inspector Lestrade, of Scotland Yard."

The mention of the metropolitan force brought an unexpected smile to her countenance. "I see. Well, you had better step in then, gentlemen."

We followed her down a narrow hallway before turning right into a small sitting room. It was a tidy but sparsely furnished room containing a settee and single armchair. At Holmes's direction, Mrs. Carrington sat in the chair, while Lestrade and I took the two-seater. Holmes continued to stand and came straight to the point. "We have reason to believe that you are acquainted with a man named Arthur Conk-Singleton?"

"*Are acquainted?*" she intoned, her accent becoming noticeably more pronounced. "Don't you mean, *were acquainted*? The guy's dead, after all."

Holmes ignored the jibe. "Perhaps you could tell us when you last saw him?"

There was no deceit in her response. "That would be the Sunday when I shot him, I guess." She reached for a small box on the walnut table beside her.

Lestrade was about to rise from the settee, but Holmes gestured for him to remain seated. "That is remarkably honest of you, Mrs. Carrington."

"*Remarkably honest?*" She opened the small box and removed from it a cigarette, which she then lit with a match. "You Englishmen have such a turn of phrase. There's no real honesty to this, just the recognition that I'm done for. I had hoped my little trip to South Kensington had gone unnoticed by Scotland Yard, but I see that is not the case. There would be no other reason for you to be here, so I see little point in denying anything. Conk-Singleton had it coming."

"...For what he did to your father, Edward Marr?"

"My word! You have done your research! Yeah, my father languished in a jail cell because of that man and was killed by another convict. Did you know that? Did you also know that Conk-Singleton double-crossed him?"

"We know that Conk-Singleton took the Ninger counterfeit as part of the deal he struck with your father."

For the first time she looked genuinely surprised. "Are you a Pinkerton man? You seem to know an awful lot about this."

"No, I'm a private detective. I'm aware of your father's long career as a forger and your own talents as plate engraver. It was you who produced the counterfeit which now sits in the Conk-Singleton collection masquerading as the work of Emanuel Ninger, wasn't it?"

"There's no stopping you, is there? Take a walk further down that hall and you'll find all the tools of my trade. I've been engraving plates in that back room for the past three years. Little good it did me. Some months I can barely afford to pay the rent."

"It would be helpful if you could tell us how you first became acquainted with Conk-Singleton."

"Now, there's a story!" She stubbed out what remained of her cigarette and reached for another. Holmes stepped forward and held out his silver case. She took one of his hand-rolled cigarettes and lit it, before continuing.

"Thank you, Sir. My father moved to this country some years ago and I came with him, my mother having passed when I was ten years old. He had always been an expert forger and hoped I would pick up the trade. But while I was a decent enough engraver, I lacked his expertise and wanted a different life. I met and fell in love with an insurance salesman called Benjamin Carrington. We married and moved to a decent property north of the river. My father understood that I wanted a stable life and went his own way.

For a while, Benjamin earned enough for us to be comfortable, but then he fell ill with consumption. Five years ago he died, leaving me alone with just a small inheritance. And after that my father was arrested.

"I moved around for some months, eventually renting this place. With the small amount of money I had left, I invested in some decent tools and began an engraving business. At first I undertook legitimate work, producing plates for the insurance company that Benjamin had worked for, but the money was poor. So I made contact with some friends of my father's and began to turn out plates for banknotes. They paid me well for a finished plate, but it was a slow process and took me weeks to complete each one. In my spare time I took to painting and sculpting, my real passions in life.

"To better understand currency design I joined the Numismatic Society of London. It gave me access to lots of banknotes, some of which I would then copy. I was something of a novelty within the society, being one of only two female members, but everyone was pleasant enough. Arthur Conk-Singleton took a particular interest in me and was always inviting me to view his collection. But I had no interest in the man or his banknotes until the day he mentioned that he had within his home a genuine Ninger counterfeit.

"I should explain that in the summer of 1889, my father spent some time in Manhattan and while there managed to obtain a twenty-dollar counterfeit produced by Emanuel Ninger. At the time it was something of a novelty, but being a traditional engraver, my father knew it was a thing of beauty. He treasured that banknote, watching the value of Ninger's work rise and believing that one day, when he came to sell it, it would enable him to escape his life of crime. While I never knew the detail of what happened, friends of my father's told me that he had been forced to give up the Ninger when he was under investigation by the Bank of England.

"My suspicions were aroused as soon as Conk-Singleton mentioned the Ninger. I knew there had to be a connection. I made some discreet enquiries at the society, asking another member about the man's earlier career. When I was told that he had worked for the Bank of England and had been responsible for investigating counterfeiters, I knew he had played some part in my father's downfall. Without giving him any hint as to my interest, I mentioned to him at one of the meetings that I would be interested in seeing his collection. He was thrilled and invited me to South Kensington that following weekend, suggesting that I should visit on the Sunday evening when his housekeeper was at church.

"I had already set my mind on taking back the Ninger and – as you have rightly ascertained, Mr. Holmes – decided to replace it with a queer note of my own. As for Conk-Singleton, he was a powerfully built man, so I was taking no chances. I packed my small handgun for protection and took a cab that afternoon.

"When I got to the High Street in South Kensington, I asked the driver to set me down a couple of streets away from Gloucester Road. I had deliberately dressed in some drab clothes and did my best to keep my face covered. I was pretty certain when I arrived at his front door, that no one had seen me.

"Conk-Singleton was charming at first and we shared a glass of Madeira wine and chatted about his collection. I asked him how he'd obtained the Ninger, acknowledging that I knew his work to be rare. What he said in response both shocked and appalled me. He said he'd been investigating a 'low-life forger who deserved the gallows' but learnt that the felon owned a genuine Ninger. He laughed as he said he'd agreed to a trade – the forgery in return for him 'putting in a good word' with the authorities, to get my father off the counterfeiting charge.

"I've been in some scrapes in my time and know just how to keep a poker face, but I'll admit, it was all I could do to keep from drawing that gun and shooting him there and then. Luckily, as I placed my glass down on his table, he suggested we go and view his collection of US counterfeits. I followed him into the room and watched as he stood before the cabinet, talking endlessly about the banknotes; how much he'd paid for each one and how much they were now worth. When he finally pointed at the Ninger, I asked if I could see it close up, to better appreciate the delicate brush work on the Treasury seal. He stepped forward and with a key he took from his waistcoat, unlocked the double-doors of the cabinet.

"I knew this would be my best opportunity and reached into my bag to retrieve the Derringer. Placing it quickly in the centre of his back I fired. Just the one shot, but enough to floor him – there was no struggle, no words, and no remorse. As I said earlier, he had it coming. I took the Ninger, substituting it with my own forged note, and headed back to the parlour, where I wiped my lipstick from the wine glass. I then left via the front door and caught a cab back home. That's the story, all told."

I cast a glance towards Lestrade, who sat open-mouthed and dazed by the disclosure. In its own way, it was one of the most chilling accounts of murder I had ever heard – that such an act could be recounted with not so much as a hint of compunction. Holmes appeared to take a very different view: "Thank you, Mrs. Carrington. That is most enlightening."

We allowed her to attend to a few domestic affairs and then waited for her to fashion her hair and retrieve a light jacket and parasol from the hallway, before accompanying her out into the street. The four of us then walked up to Borough High Street to hail a suitable carriage for the trip to Scotland Yard.

It was not our finest case, but it was one that Inspector Lestrade was often to reflect on as we sat together in the upstairs room of 221B. For the Conk-Singleton murder, Mrs. Jean Carrington was to face the gallows in the prison yard of Newgate on a particular cold November morning. Her final words to the chaplain were, "I wish to die, as I have lived, without regret. But I hope my place in Heaven is assured."

Notes: As a result of time earned for good behaviour, Emanuel Ninger was eventually released from the Erie County Penitentiary in July 1900, a few months after our investigation of the Conk-Singleton case. He was told officially that he still faced two indictments, although later that year these were marked *nolle prosequi* by the US Attorney, who announced that he did not intend to prosecute the case against Ninger. As far as is known, Ninger never returned to counterfeiting.

It was not until the passing of an Act on the 4th March 1909, that American residents were required to turn over all counterfeit currency and stamps to the US Treasury. Since that time, the Secret Service has been active in tracking down and destroying counterfeit US notes wherever they are held. The Conk-Singleton forgeries eventually met the same fate, except for one. The remarkable twenty-dollar bill produced with such care by Emanuel Ninger stills sits on display within the Black Museum of Scotland Yard. – JHW.

8. The Stratford Poisoner

 M y colleague had been working in his makeshift laboratory for a good twenty minutes. In that time he had said nothing, absorbed as he was with his apparatus, pouring different chemicals into the rack of test-tubes and glass flasks set out on the bench before him. He turned to me suddenly.

"It is attempted murder, Watson – without doubt, attempted murder!"

I looked up from my book. "What is?"

"I first tested for a base which I thought might be arsenic. The Reinsch test gave me unequivocal evidence of the poison. To be certain, I used this apparatus for the Marsh test. I was able to produce its metallic state both times, so I am certain that white arsenic trioxide – or *poudre de succession* as the French like to call it – has to be present. Somebody has set out to kill me!"

Shocked by this surprise disclosure, I placed the book down on the sofa and gave him my full attention. "You'll have to explain, what has happened?"

"I received an unexpected gift early this afternoon, a small bottle of single malt whisky produced by the Lea Valley Distillery. It was addressed to me and packaged in a wooden box, but came with no letter or greetings card. Naturally, I was suspicious, and a close examination of the cork stopper revealed that the bottle had been tampered with. While I could detect no particular odour beyond the distinctive peaty bouquet of the whisky, I recognised that this would be the perfect medium for dispensing a toxic agent. I therefore set out to confirm my suspicions, focusing first on white arsenic, that most fashionable of poisons. And the results have proved positive!"

"That is extremely worrying," said I. "Do you have any idea who might have sent it?"

"We will come to that. I should first take you through the clues as they presented themselves. Firstly, the bottle itself – a reasonably expensive malt with many features to commend it. The half-size bottle and presentation box tells us that it was designed to be given as a gift. Therefore, the perfect choice for our would-be poisoner, who hoped that I would be delighted to receive it and eager to sample its contents. The distillery's name, crest and address have been stamped on the lid of the box using a branding iron."

"Is that significant?" I asked.

"In this case, yes. A quick look at my trade directories, and some of the advertisements they contain, was most enlightening. The distillery is based in Stratford and sits on the banks of the Lea River, its malt being transported from a warehouse in Hertfordshire. It has modelled itself on some of the best Scottish distilleries and produces more than 100,000 gallons of malt whisky each year, in addition to a significant quantity of grain whisky. While its spirits are sold in outlets all over the capital, these presentation boxes can only be purchased from the factory site."

"So you're thinking that the purchaser is a regular whisky drinker who lives in the vicinity of the distillery?"

"Both are but possibilities at this stage, but I would suggest that they give us some early steps towards a working hypothesis. Now, let us focus on the method of delivery." He reached to his side and held up a folded sheaf of brown paper.

"The box was enveloped in this thick wrapping paper and tied with string. The paper had been reused and had no doubt once covered a different parcel. While the sender had been careful to ensure that no address details remained – by removing the top of three original sheets of wrapping paper - they had not been overly meticulous. A close examination revealed there to be a small, but telling, impression of the original hand-written address beneath the label applied to this parcel. While only three characters could be discerned, these were, I believe, the final three letters of the address. They read '...*ord*'.

"Consistent with the sender being based in *Stratford*!" I intoned.

"Precisely. It lends further weight to our initial theory. The paper and address label had been stuck down with some cheap paper glue. Unfortunately, I could not determine the manufacturer. However, the string used to secure the package revealed two features of interest. Firstly, it had been cut with a blunt knife. The frayed edges demonstrated that the knife did not cut through the twine cleanly in one go, but had been used rather to *saw* through the strands. So our sender is no office worker with a handy pair of sharp scissors. Secondly, the nature of the string itself; it was an unusually thick twine. In practical terms, it looked more like the sort of cord that would be used for gardening or building purposes – to lay out a row of plants perhaps, or to secure a plumb-line."

"Again, suggestive of someone who works in a trade, rather than an office."

"Yes, and there were a few other clues to support such an assertion. I found a smudged thumbprint on the bottom left corner of the package. The look and smell of the residue suggested some form of bitumen, like the black pitch used to stain the wooden walls of agricultural or industrial buildings. The address label had been typed, yet the sender was no typist, as there were two characters mistyped and corrected. And all of the usual niceties around the form of address had been ignored – the name on the parcel reading simply as 'Sherlock Holmes' with no added 'Mr.' or 'Esquire'."

I pointed out one obvious observation. "Ah, but the sender must have had *access* to a typewriter."

Holmes grinned. "Agreed! And someone who was keen to avoid presenting me with a *handwritten* address."

"Well, that would be a fairly damning clue if the matter were to be investigated."

"True, but I am convinced in this case that it is suggestive of something broader. Principally, that the sender feared I might be able to recognise the handwriting and would therefore be suspicious of the gift. In other words, the poisoner is someone we have investigated in the past."

It was my turn to smile. "That's no great revelation. I had assumed that from the start!"

"Yes, but it should help to narrow down our list of suspects. Now, one of the final clues came from the posting of the package." Once more he held up the sheaf of wrapping paper. "You can see the date and postmark. The package was taken this morning to a post office in central London. And yet, Stratford has its own post office and there are plenty of private delivery firms in that part of the East End."

"Well, I'm guessing that the sender was again trying to disguise the fact that the parcel had started its journey in Stratford."

"Correct. And another indication that they live in Stratford, for the Great Eastern Railway line passes through the town on its way to Liverpool Street Station. The post office is the one closest to the terminal. Misdirection certainly, but perhaps the sender is also somebody who regularly travels up to town as part of his trade."

Holmes moved away from the laboratory and retrieved a small cigar box from the mantelpiece. A short while later we were both smoking fine Havana cigars and I took the opportunity to review what we had learnt so far. "Then our mystery character is a whisky-drinking tradesman, living in Stratford, with access to a typewriter, who may travel regularly by train to London as part of his work."

He sent a plume of grey smoke high into the air. "Most certainly, and I think you are right to suggest that it is a *man* given the size of the thumbprint I found on the parcel."

"Where does that leave us? Given the profile I have just outlined, it could still be a very long list of potential suspects if you consider the wide variety of murderers, thieves, swindlers and gangsters you have encountered over the years."

My colleague smirked. "So far, I have run through only the *observations* I have made and some rudimentary deductions, some of which might prove to be erroneous. Now we must apply some knowledge and evaluate what we have. My first contention is that our man must have a strong desire to seek *revenge* for something I have done. Perhaps as a result of my intervention in his affairs he suffered a loss; a loss of his liberty or property, maybe even the loss of a loved one. If we cast our minds back, there could be a fair number of those, but how many have made a *specific* threat against me?"

"There have been quite a few."

"Ah, but who was it who said, 'I have to thank you for a good deal. Perhaps I'll pay my debt someday.'"

I was slow in recalling the character, but eventually hit upon the name. "Oldacre!" I cried, "Yes, Jonas Oldacre – the 'Norwood Builder'!"

"Ha! You have it. Now, a little more information will add to the overall picture. You will recollect that when we left the case in the hands of Inspector Lestrade, it was his belief that Oldacre would face a charge of conspiracy for attempting to defraud his creditors by pretending to be dead and making it appear as if the young solicitor, John Hector McFarlane, had murdered him. It may interest you to know that when he eventually went to trial, in the November of '94, it was not for the charge of conspiracy."

"Really?"

"There was some concern that it might be difficult to prove conspiracy, when the act is generally seen as an agreement between two or more people to commit a criminal offence. Jonas Oldacre had operated alone and McFarlane was merely an innocent man caught up in the overall scheme. The prosecution's case rested firmly on the fraud that had been perpetrated and creditors' loss of many thousands of pounds. Oldacre was found guilty and sentenced to seven years in Wandsworth. Declared bankrupt, he was also forced to sell Deep Dene House and all of his land in Lower Norwood."

"He may well have a desire to seek revenge, Holmes, but if he is serving a seven year stretch that would mean he is due to be released in November 1901 – one year and three months from now. It cannot be he!"

Holmes clapped his hands together and leapt up from his chair with boyish enthusiasm. "It can! Some weeks back, I had occasion to speak to Inspector Lestrade in wrapping up some of the details of the Conk-Singleton forgery case. Just before I left him, he made reference to the 'Norwood Builder' and said that Oldacre had received an unexpected *ticket of leave* for his exemplary behaviour as a prisoner. He was released from Wandsworth in early July. There was one condition attached to his release; that he was not to go back and reside, or carry on any sort of business, in Lower Norwood."

"Fascinating. So it may be that he has relocated to Stratford and resumed work as a builder."

"That would seem to fit the facts. It just remains for us to confirm whether we have correctly interpreted the clues or are just barking up the wrong tree!"

****

The following evening we took the short rail journey from Liverpool Street Station to Stratford. Holmes had been busy during the day finding out more about Jonas Oldacre's release from Wandsworth. A quick telegram to the prison governor had brought a most helpful response. As part of the release process, Oldacre had been required to inform the authorities where he planned to reside. It was no great surprise to learn that the address he had given was in Stratford.

The mid-terraced house on Vaughan Road was around a mile from the railway station. It was nearly six-thirty as we approached the dark blue door of the property. Holmes raised the brass door knocker and used it to announce our arrival. It took some time for the knock to be answered. When the latch was finally released and the door swung open, we were greeted by a thin, gaunt-faced man with thinning white hair and deep-set grey eyes. There was no mistaking the ferret-like features of Jonas Oldacre, but the spell in prison had aged him way beyond his fifty-eight years. He looked confused for a brief moment and then gave us a thin, and wholly unexpected, smile.

"Good evening, gentlemen! I had hoped for a response from you, Mr. Holmes, but did not imagine for one moment that you would visit me. Please step in."

I was completely bewildered. There appeared to be no animosity in his tone and having stepped back from the door to welcome us in to the house, Oldacre directed us towards the front sitting room. Holmes responded with evident aplomb: "Thank you, Mr. Oldacre. That is most kind of you."

We found ourselves in a dingy room brim full of furniture and detritus. Some bedding was laid out on the floor along one wall. In a corner opposite was a partially obscured wooden table and thin-legged chair covered in newspapers and piles of paperwork. I saw Holmes's gaze fall upon a battered looking typewriter which was also hidden within the rammel. The only window in the room looked out onto the street and was bedecked with heavy red cloth drapes and filthy, dirt-stained, net curtains. While there were three chairs within the space, all were covered in clothes, boots and tools. Oldacre apologised for the mess, explaining that he rented but the one room in the house.

Like me, Holmes had seemed content to let Oldacre take the lead to this point, but interjected suddenly. "How have you been since leaving prison?"

Oldacre gave him a doleful expression and shook his head slowly. "Not good, Mr. Holmes. I will be honest in saying that I have struggled. I'm grateful to have this roof over my head and pay only three shillings a week for the room, but have not been able to secure much work." He pointed towards the wooden table. "I've been trying to set up a new building firm, but the paperwork is overwhelming me and some of my old contacts are reluctant to employ an ex-convict, as I'm sure you'll understand. To bring in something of an income, I've been forced to work as a bricklayer, travelling into town for part of each week. That was the reason for my gift to you. I imagine you may feel it was irregular on my part, but I hoped you would be able to forgive me and help me to earn an honest living."

Holmes showed little reaction and changed tack. "I see. So it was you that sent me the bottle?"

Oldacre looked slightly unsettled. "Yes. I'm no drinker these days, so the whisky was no use to me. I thought that's why you'd called on me. How else did you know where I was living?"

I took it upon myself to intervene. "Mr. Oldacre, forgive me, but there seems to be some confusion here. Yesterday, Mr. Holmes received through the post a small bottle of whisky in a wooden box. It was clearly addressed to him, but contained no note or other indication as to the sender. It was only as a result of my colleague's investigative abilities that he was able to identify you as the person most likely to have sent it." I chose my words carefully so as not to reveal more at this stage.

"Then there is certainly something amiss, gentlemen. I wrote a letter to Mr. Holmes explaining that while in prison I underwent something of an epiphany. I realised what a contemptable character I had been in my life and, with time to reflect on such matters, took to re-reading the gospel. With the support of the prison chaplain I have set myself on a path to righteousness – a conversion that helped secure me an early release from Wandsworth. I expressed my apologies to you, Mr. Holmes, for threatening you the way I did when we last met. I also sent a similar letter to the solicitor, John McFarlane, for the mistreatment he received at my hands."

This time it was Holmes who looked to be choosing his words very cautiously. "Did you also send Mr. McFarlane a bottle of that fine whisky?"

Oldacre beamed. "I did indeed! I hoped it might draw a line in the sand, so to speak, and enable you both to forgive me. Beyond that, it was my broader wish that if you had any useful contacts through which I might secure work, I would be delighted to hear from you."

There was an uneasy silence. I knew not what to say nor how to react to his account. I imagined that Holmes felt similarly tongue-tied. With Oldacre clearly looking for one of us to respond in some way, I seized the initiative: "Mr. Oldacre, I must leave you in Holmes's capable hands, as I have a private patient to attend to. It could be a matter of life or death."

Holmes comprehended my meaning immediately and played along with the ruse. "Yes, thank you, Watson. I would also be grateful if you could get a message to our friends to say that I may be detained here for a short while, but look forward to seeing them later." I knew this was his coded request for me to contact Scotland Yard. I said my goodbyes and wasted no time in heading back towards the railway station.

I was unsure initially how to go about finding John McFarlane, given the passage of years since the original case I had documented as *The Adventure of the Norwood Builder*. I recollected that while the young solicitor had lived with his parents in Blackheath, he had worked as a junior partner in a law firm near Holborn Viaduct. Faced with the prospect of a lengthy journey south of the river or a quick cab ride to the nearby offices of Graham and McFarlane at 426, Gresham Buildings, I opted for the latter. Before hailing a cab on Sun Street, I used the telegraph office at the station to send a short telegram to Inspector Lestrade requesting that he send a couple of officers to Stratford to assist Holmes.

When I stepped down from the cab outside the offices of the law firm, I was reassured to see that there were still many lights on in the four storey building. I was greeted at the door by a uniformed concierge who could not have been more helpful when I explained that I needed to contact John Hector McFarlane on a matter of some urgency. He wasted no time in escorting me into the building and up to the first floor, where he said that Mr. McFarlane had his own private office. It was a matter of some relief to learn that the fair-haired solicitor was not only still at work, but also appeared to be in the best of health, being a little more thickset than I remembered him and sporting a full beard.

McFarlane was delighted, if not a little bemused, to receive me at that hour. He said he had been made a senior partner within the firm, so working late was not uncommon, and then asked how life was treating me and inquired after Holmes. With the formalities dealt with, I went on to explain the reason for my call, telling him first that Jonas Oldacre had been released from prison earlier than expected.

"Thank you, Doctor, although I have to confess that I was aware of his early remission. A barrister friend in my local lodge told me the news a few weeks back. I was not particularly concerned as I imagined he posed no further threat. My mother died earlier this year, so he can no longer trouble her either."

After offering my condolences, I then moved on to the issue of the parcel. "This may seem like a strange question,

Mr. McFarlane, but have you recently received a package containing a small bottle of whisky?"

He raised his eyebrows in mock surprise. "I did! Are you going to tell me that you or Mr. Holmes sent it? I have been curious to know who the sender was, as the parcel arrived with no accompanying paperwork."

"I have to tell you that it was Jonas Oldacre who sent it, as a *gift*."

He looked at me very directly as if seeking some further clarification, and then asked, "Why would he do that?"

"Possibly to poison you."

The colour drained from McFarlane's face. There was no disguising his look of fear. With some trepidation I posed the critical question. "What did you do with the bottle? Please tell me that you didn't drink any of it?"

"No...No, luckily I placed it to one side. I still have it in the drawer beside me." He reached to his left and retrieved the bottle, setting it on the desk before him and handling it as if it were about to explode.

"I would be grateful if you could retain the bottle. It will need to be tested by the police toxicologist."

"Of course," he replied.

I spent the next ten minutes telling him all about the poisoned bottle that Holmes had received and the clues that had pointed us towards Oldacre. When he then heard about the early evening encounter with the builder, he was thoroughly perturbed. "Do you think he's lost his mind?"

"It's hard to know. He seemed sincere, but may be suffering from some form of psychosis or *dissociation*. Prison can do that occasionally, leading some inmates to believe they have committed no crime at all. I suspect the police will want to have him thoroughly examined by a Home Office doctor. Whether this episode results in any charges being brought against him remains to be seen. At the very least, I would imagine that he will be returned to prison or detained in a criminal lunatic asylum."

There was little more to discuss, so I thanked McFarlane for his time and indicated that the police were likely to want to interview him the next day. He said he would rearrange some of his planned appointments to provide for this. He then walked me down to the ground floor of the building and accompanied me out onto the street, expressing his gratitude for what I had done in preventing him from being poisoned.

****

It was a little beyond midnight when I finally heard Holmes's footfall on the stairs. He looked tired but cheery as he entered the apartment. Having removed his jacket and travelling cap he slumped into an armchair and reached for his briar pipe. "Well, well, Watson. How did you get on with McFarlane? I trust he is alive and well?"

I relayed to him the gist of my conversation with the solicitor and he thanked me for my quick thinking back at Vaughan Road. I was reassured to hear that my telegram to Scotland Yard had led to two police constables being dispatched to the address.

"Presumably, they now have Oldacre under lock and key?" It was more of a statement than a question, so it came as something of a surprise when my colleague answered in the negative.

"Hardly, Watson! They spent some time getting a statement from him, but then proceeded to arrest and handcuff the real culprit in the case."

My surprise was palpable. "What *culprit*?"

"Why, Mrs. Lexington, of course – Oldacre's former housekeeper from Deep Dene House."

"Mrs. Lexington? What has this got to do with her?"

Holmes pointed the stem of his pipe towards me. "The Vaughan Road house is hers. It had once been owned by Oldacre, who gifted the property to her some months before he faced the fraud charges. It was a reward for her loyalty and also enabled him to stop the property falling into the hands of his creditors. When he learnt of his early release, Oldacre wrote to Lexington asking if she could take him in for a short while until his new building venture was up and running."

"Did you know all of this before we set out this evening?"

"No. But I realised as soon as we arrived at Vaughan Road that something was amiss. The house had some distinctive feminine flourishes. When Oldacre said he rented just the one room, I thought it likely that he was sharing the property with a landlady. A quick look at some of the correspondence beside the typewriter on his table revealed her name."

"Why should any of her letters be in his room?" I enquired.

"Because she had been acting as his unpaid secretary, typing letters in order to help him re-establish the building business."

"Ah ha! So she typed the label on your parcel."

"Precisely. She is no typist, but was doing all she could to help her former employer."

"That I can comprehend, but I still do not understand why she took it upon herself to try to kill you and McFarlane. Was this, again, some misguided loyalty on her part?"

Holmes waved his head slowly from side to side. "Far from it, my friend. This crime was all of her doing. Oldacre had no knowledge of what was planned and she acted to incriminate him."

"Remarkable. So how did you find all this out?"

"After you left, I asked Oldacre about his landlady. He confirmed that Mrs. Lexington had taken him in. At first she had been only too pleased to help and was initially reluctant to charge him any rent. He admitted that everything seemed to change as soon as he told her about his newfound religious conviction. And it all started with the whisky.

"When they had resided at Deep Dene House, Oldacre had been something of a connoisseur of English whisky. In preparing for his release from prison, Mrs. Lexington had taken it upon herself to visit the local Lea Valley Distillery to purchase two bottles of expensive whisky as a homecoming gift. But when she presented these to Oldacre, he explained that he wanted to keep to his pledge as a teetotaller. She was most affronted and began to grow increasingly indifferent as he struggled to find work. When he was forced to take the bricklaying job, she announced that he would have to start paying rent.

"Most evenings Mrs. Lexington walks into town to do a couple of hours' clerical work for a local undertaker. Very occasionally, she is required to type letters, but being no typist, asked her employer some time ago if she could take the typewriter home, so that she could work on these in her own time, rather than his. The arrangement worked well for Mrs. Lexington who was then able to work on the letters at her leisure, while learning to become a more proficient clerk typist. When we called this evening, she was at her place of work.

"Having heard this new information from Oldacre, I was convinced that Mrs. Lexington had played some part in the affair. From his general demeanour, it was clear that the builder had not yet realised that anything untoward had occurred. I asked him to describe how the idea of sending the packages had come about and the process by which he had despatched the bottles. His testimony was most revealing.

"Mrs. Lexington had declared one evening – somewhat out of the blue – that as a decent Christian, Oldacre ought to make amends for his earlier misdeeds and write an apology to all of those he had wronged in the past. She suggested that he might wish to start with Mr. McFarlane and me, as she had already obtained our addresses. She further proposed that each letter be accompanied by a gift of some kind. In the case of these two initial apologies, why not make use of the superfluous whisky which Mr. Oldacre had declared he was unable to consume? Oldacre felt it to be a splendid idea and set to work on the letters. Mrs. Lexington agreed to type out some address labels while he was doing this.

"When the letters were completed, Mrs. Lexington took charge and said that she would wrap the parcels with some paper she had kept from an earlier package. This she did in her own parlour unseen by Oldacre."

I interposed at this point. "So she had already poisoned the whisky and wrapped the parcels without including the letters?"

"Yes. And when she returned them to Oldacre, she suggested that he further secure each with some twine that sat on a chair in his room."

"Further implicating Oldacre!"

"You have it, Watson. All of this was designed to point the finger at him. It mattered not to her whether the deed resulted in murder or merely an accusation of attempted murder. She knew that the newly released Oldacre would be a prime suspect in either case, and all of the clues would point to him. She added to this by suggesting that he post the parcels on his next rail trip into London."

"Astonishing! But *why* did she do it?"

"The answer to that came when Mrs. Lexington returned home at about nine-thirty. By then Lestrade's men had joined me at the house and I was forced to disclose my suspicions, both to them and Oldacre. Only then did he realise he had been duped by his once-loyal housekeeper. He provided the police with a full statement of what he had already told me.

"Mrs. Lexington was shocked to find the police officers waiting for her when she let herself into the house. Asked to step into Oldacre's room, she saw both he and I seated and became instantly petulant, at first refusing to acknowledge that she had played any part in the affair. But as I began to go through the evidence her jaw was set hard and her dark eyes filled with hatred.

"'Damn you!' she cried. 'I don't know who I loathe more – you, the pompous overblown detective, with his snooty ways and interfering manner, or *him*.' She pointed at Oldacre, who appeared almost childlike as he looked towards her in disbelief. 'See what *he* has become? A snivelling little shadow of his former self. Preaching and picking away at me with his holier-than-thou attitude yet unable to fend for himself. I was once proud to call him my master and I stuck by him. He repaid me with this house, which at first I thought I might be happy to share with him. But I cannot reconcile myself with what he has become. And I blame you and that interfering McFarlane for this. I had hoped to get rid of all three of you.'

"She fell silent at that point and her head dropped. For some moments she steadfastly refused to look at Oldacre, who still sat staring and open-mouthed. As one of the constables stepped forward to handcuff her, she raised her head defiantly and gave Oldacre a withering stare, before turning and being led away. I imagine she is now enjoying the hospitality of a police cell in Bow Street and thereafter can expect to be moved to Holloway."

"What about Oldacre?" I queried. "What will happen to him?"

"I left him alone in the house. He said he would spend one more night there, but planned to leave the next day. Since moving to Stratford he has been attending the Highway Church on Romford Road and felt certain that the local vicar would help him to find alternative accommodation. I believe the man has undergone a genuine transformation."

"Wonders will never cease, Holmes! Who'd have thought it – the reappearance of the Norwood Builder! I might have to write that up one day."

"Well, I will leave that to you, dear friend," was all that he added.

To my knowledge, we never discussed the case again. And it was quickly forgotten at the time, for the following day we became embroiled in a major international crisis which threatened to destabilise the monarchy of a leading European power. As for Mr. Jonas Oldacre, I did learn, sometime later, that he had taken to missionary work in East Africa with some evident success. Perhaps, in the eyes of the Lord, he did indeed pay back his debt.